Hurry up and fetch all of the Good Dogs adventures!

GOOD DOGS
with BAD HAIRCUTS

Rachel Wenitsky & David Sidorov

illustrated by Tor Freeman

G. P. PUTNAM'S SONS

An imprint of Penguin Random House LLC, New York

Text copyright © 2021 by Working Partners Ltd.
Illustrations copyright © 2021 by Victoria Freeman

G. P. Putnam's Sons is a registered trademark of Penguin Random House LLC.

Visit us online at penguinrandomhouse.com

Library of Congress Cataloging-in-Publication Data
Names: Sidorov, David, author. | Wenitsky, Rachel, author. | Freeman, Tor, illustrator.
Title: Good dogs with bad haircuts / David Sidorov and Rachel Wenitsky; illustrated by Tor Freeman.
Description: New York: G. P. Putnam's Sons, [2021] | Series: [Good dogs; 2] | Summary: "The Good Dogs must come together when a special neighborhood wedding is on the brink of disaster"—Provided by publisher.
Identifiers: LCCN 2020010474 (print) | LCCN 2020010475 (ebook) | ISBN 9780593108475 | ISBN 9780593108482 (ebook)
Subjects: CYAC: Dogs—Fiction. | Behavior—Fiction. | Weddings—Fiction.
Classification: LCC PZ7.1.S526 Gow 2021 (print) | LCC PZ7.1.S526 (ebook) | DDC [Fic]—dc23
LC record available at https://lccn.loc.gov/2020010474
LC ebook record available at https://lccn.loc.gov/2020010475

Printed in Canada
ISBN 9780593108475

1 3 5 7 9 10 8 6 4 2

Design by Eileen Savage and Suki Boynton
Text set in Chaparral Pro, Archer, and Johnston ITC Pro

For Molly, Freddie, Whiskey, and Rosie
—R.W. and D.S.

For dear Auntie Kate and her Gus!
Love from Tor xx

CHAPTER 1

Grass! Dirt! Trash can! Stick! Grass! Trash! Human leg! King had a lot of favorite things, and the park was home to most of them. He darted around excitedly, smelling the familiar smells, then stopped suddenly in his tracks.

"A leaf! Leaf! Look at this leaf! Check it out! A leaf!" King wagged his tail wildly as he shouted to Lulu and Hugo. He knew that the humans in the dog run just heard a series of excited barks and yelps, but his friends understood.

"Seems like King really loves that leaf," Lulu said. She was sitting under a tree, biting into a chew toy shaped like a designer handbag.

King inched closer to the leaf, stuck out his nose, and took in a big whiff. *Mmm,* he thought. *There's nothing like the smell of a red leaf sprinkled with a little bit of dirt and pee in the morning!*

"Stick! Stick! Stick! Check it out! A stick!"

King turned to see Waffles the puppy running toward him, carrying a stick that was bigger than her whole body.

Ohhh yeah, he thought. *Definitely gonna play with that.*

"Careful with that thing, Waff!" Hugo called out to his new younger sister. He and Napoleon were racing each other across the fenced-in area, both chasing the same ball that Erin had thrown. But King noticed that even while Hugo was playing, he always had a watchful eye on Waffles.

"I'm serious, Waffles!" Hugo warned as he stopped running. "You could hurt somebody with that thing!"

"Zoe lets me play with big sticks all the time!" Waffles yelped.

"I love Zoe as much as you do, but you have to remember that she's a five-year-old human and I'm an *eight*-year-old dog, so I think I know a little bit more—"

"Ha! Ya snooze, ya lose!" Napoleon barked, grabbing the ball and bumping Hugo with his rear end as he swiveled to sprint back to Erin. She was King's owner and his favorite human in the world. She also ran Good Dogs doggy day care, so she was keeping an eye on all of his friends—including Cleo, his big sister, a German shepherd mix, who was diligently running laps. She was so fast that nobody could catch up with her.

King and Waffles tumbled in the dirt, chewing on opposite ends of the stick. They were playing a game they had recently invented called the Stick Game, which involved tumbling in the dirt and chewing on opposite ends of a stick. King felt like he was a little better at the Stick Game, since he was a *slightly* older puppy than Waffles—not to mention, he had recently gotten fifth place in an agility contest. It wasn't perfect, but fifth was a lot better than dead last! And who needed to be *perfect*? He had also been the runner-up for "Most Improved." King wasn't sure what *runner-up* meant, but assumed that he'd gotten that because he loved to run and jump.

After they were done, Waffles started wrestling with Petunia, and King hopped onto the bench where Erin was sitting, plopped his head in her lap, and got some really great pets. As he looked out at the other dogs, King thought, *This is just about as good as it gets.* All of his friends *and* family in one place.

Cleo and Erin were his family, but when he really thought about it, his friends were kind of like his family too. And these days, it was pretty rare that they were all together at the park! Lulu had been going to the set of Jasmine's movie most days, living what King imagined was a very elegant movie-star life. He had eaten enough entertainment magazines to know that Hollywood seemed glamorous and fun (and that paper was delicious). He didn't know much, but he assumed a movie set probably had *hundreds* of entertainment magazines to eat.

"How come you aren't on your movie set today?" he called over to Lulu.

"Jasmine has the day off, and she had to go to some meetings," she replied, scratching her silky Yorkie ear with her manicured paw. "But I think we're about to get a lot busier! Jasmine thinks she might get to be in the *sequel*."

"What's a sequel?" King asked.

"It's sort of like another story that's even better than the first one!" Lulu said.

"That sounds great. I love sequels," King said. Then there was a series of loud, booming barks—and the dogs turned to see that they belonged to Napoleon.

"Hey, lady! Hey, lady! Gimme some of those chips! I want chips!"

Napoleon was barking his demands at a woman on a bench who was eating some particularly delicious-smelling potato chips. He was staring into her eyes. Clearly, he meant business.

"Napoleon," Erin said sternly but kindly. "Leave the nice lady alone."

"He's come a long way," Cleo said to Lulu, and King turned to listen. "A few weeks ago, he would have jumped onto that woman's lap and snatched the chips right out of her hand. Amazing what behavior training and a couple of days a week at Good Dogs will do."

It was true, King thought. Barking nonstop at a stranger in the park wasn't exactly *great* behavior, but for Napoleon, it was terrific! Ever since the day when King, Lulu, and Hugo had met Waffles and rescued Napoleon, the rebellious French bulldog had been coming to Good Dogs and seeing a special trainer, and it seemed like it was really making a difference. King had a feeling Napoleon's family was paying more attention to him too. But Napoleon heard Cleo's comment and turned to bark at her.

"I could steal her chips if I wanted to!" Napoleon

insisted. "I steal chips all the time. I just don't feel like it right now."

Then King heard something very familiar.

"I think they're probably under the elm tree, Nuts," Lulu said patiently.

She was helping their squirrel friend find his acorn stash. King, Hugo, and Waffles walked over to join the conversation. King loved helping Nuts find his nuts because there was always the possibility that anything involving the squirrel could turn into a thrilling chase.

"I don't think they're under the elm tree. I would remember that," Nuts said, pacing nervously.

"Would you? Really?" Hugo replied skeptically.

"Listen, you guys really gotta help me out here," Nuts said, lowering his voice. "You see that beautiful female over there?"

"The one with the chips?" King asked. "Or do you mean Erin?"

"No! Not the human! The squirrel! On the fence!"

The dogs turned to see a squirrel on the fence, holding an acorn and minding her own business.

"That's Berries," Nuts gushed dreamily. "I think she's *fantastic*, don't you?"

"Uhhh . . . ," the dogs said in unison. King wasn't sure what made a squirrel fantastic.

"She loves acorns. So I collected a whole big stash to show her, but I can't remember where I put them!"

"Listen, Nuts," Lulu said. "Why don't you check the elm tree, just so you can say that you did, and we'll brainstorm some other places they could be?"

"Okay! Fine!" Nuts replied, scampering reluctantly toward the elm tree. "But the nuts aren't going to be there, and it'll be a waste of time, and then I'll have to— Oh, here they are! You were right!"

The nuts were, as always, under the elm tree. Nuts cleared his throat and stood up to face the squirrel on the fence.

"Excuse me, Berries? Would you like to see some acorns?"

Berries sighed, then slowly headed to the elm tree.

"You can have some if you want," Nuts offered nervously.

"Cute," Berries said. "But I have my own."

She hopped confidently to the other side of the elm tree, and Nuts followed. King watched as Berries showed off her own stash of acorns, which was *much* bigger. King didn't really get what was so great about acorns—they were too small to play with, and every time he tried to eat one, he barfed—but the squirrels seemed to love them.

Nuts stared at Berries's acorn pile. "Wow! You have so many. *And* you remembered where you put them. You're *fantastic!*"

"I know," Berries replied, and hopped back up to her perch on the fence.

Nuts scurried over to the dogs. "Seems like it'll take more than that to impress her," he said. "By the way, I know you just told me, but I forget, where did I put my—?"

King didn't hear the rest, because just then, the sweetest voice in the world—Erin's voice, of course—called his name and the names of all of his friends.

"King! Hugo! Lulu! Waffles! Napoleon! Petunia! Patches! Cleo! Time to go!"

The dogs lined up, ready for their leashes, and King got excited for the walk back through the neighborhood to Erin's house. Just as Erin was about to attach his leash, King smelled something familiar.

What is that? King thought, bolting away from Erin, sniffing around for the source. It smelled like something King liked a lot . . . something that was usually only at home. *Is it cheese? No. Is it a toy? No. Is it my bed?* Hmm, no. Whatever it was, it was getting closer to the park.

"Cleo?" King turned to his sister. "Don't you think that smells sort of like—?"

"Jin?!" Erin said as the gate opened and Jin walked toward them. "Babe, what are you doing here?"

"Jin? Who's Jin?!" Waffles asked, just excited to see a new person.

"Erin's boyfriend," Cleo replied. She looked just as surprised as King felt.

"Ooooh," whined Petunia with a smile.

"But what's he doing *here*?" Cleo echoed Erin's question. King wondered the same thing as he jumped up and pawed at Jin's leg. Jin was usually at work by now and never came to the dog park.

"I had a lunch break and figured I'd swing by . . . ," Jin started to say. King noticed that Cleo, who was usually so stoic and calm, had started excitedly wagging her tail.

King didn't know what was going on. He thought Jin seemed a little more nervous and weird than usual—he was sweating a lot, and he kept rubbing his palms on his pants. King was getting better at detecting human body language, and he was often nervous and weird himself, so he was extra skilled at noticing those things in others.

Then Jin dug into his pocket, and King eagerly jumped up on his hind legs.

"Your pocket! Wow, wow, wow!" King yelped. "I wonder if you brought a squeaky ball!"

"Come on, silly. Why would Jin have a—" Cleo started. But when Jin's hand came out of his pocket, she went quiet, and King went berserk. It *was* a squeaky ball! And it looked pretty bouncy too.

"OH MY DOG! OH MY DOG! OH MY DOG!" King shouted. "Cleo! I was right! It's a squeaky ball!"

The other dogs started barking happily too, but suddenly King's tail dropped in confusion. This was strange—Jin never played with squeaky balls!

Sometimes when he came over to their house, he would put the squeaky balls up on a high shelf because he didn't like the sound of them squeaking. King liked Jin, but he always thought that was odd, since everyone loved the sweet, sweet sound of a squeak.

But King didn't have much time to be confused, because now Jin was kneeling down next to him, bringing the ball right up to his nose. King realized it wasn't just *any* squeaky ball—it was the kind that usually had a T-R-E-A-T *inside* of it. King's favorite. There were two things that he loved most in the world: toys and snacks. And when one was inside of the other, oh boy, did that make him happy. King's tail started wagging so fast, it shook the rest of his body.

"Okay, buddy," Jin said softly to King. "Remember what we practiced?"

King thought about it for a moment, but he couldn't remember anything particularly noteworthy that had happened before that morning. Then: SQUEAK! SQUEAK! Jin squeezed the ball twice and gave it a good, hard toss into the air. And just like that, King was OFF! He bolted in the direction of the ball, leaped up in the air, and caught it in his mouth before it hit the ground.

Erin and Jin started clapping.

"Nice catch, King!" Hugo barked.

"Not bad!" Cleo said. "Looks like agility training is paying off."

Jin patted his leg, motioning for King to come back with the ball. But King couldn't resist the moment—he did a happy dance, wiggling his tail and running around proudly. It wasn't every day you made a perfect catch on a perfect ball, after all. He gave the ball in his mouth a few loving squeaks.

Ah, the most beautiful sound on earth, King thought as he finally trotted back over to Jin like the good boy he was. He briefly set the ball down so he could sniff it, trying to figure out what was inside it this time. Sometimes it was peanut butter, sometimes it was chicken, sometimes it was cheese! But whatever was in there that morning didn't smell like any food he knew. As he put it back in his mouth and walked toward Jin, he noticed it was making a strange sound when it moved, like *JANGLE JANGLE.*

Hmm . . . must be a special jangly treat, King thought. As he got back to his people, Jin seemed nervous again. He motioned for King to go to Erin instead.

"Jin, what are you doing?" Erin asked.

Simple, King thought. *He's playing fetch with me!*

"What's going on, babe?" Erin continued as she kneeled down to pet King. "Seriously, did you skip work?"

"Look inside the ball," Jin replied. Erin took the ball out of King's mouth.

That's strange, thought King. *Is the special jangly treat for Erin and not for me?*

"I don't see anything . . . ," Erin said, peering into it.

"What?! Really?! Uh-oh," Jin said in a panic. He looked at King in horror, then grabbed him by the collar and pulled him closer. Suddenly King felt Jin's fingers in his mouth, fishing and poking around. *What's going on?*

"Where is it, King?" Jin was raising his voice now. "Cough it up! Cough it up!"

Cough what up? King felt like this was turning into a very bizarre game of fetch.

Then Erin screamed! A happy scream! And Jin took his hand out of King's mouth.

"OHMYGOSH!" Erin exclaimed, and she pulled what looked like a sparkly little toy out of the middle of the ball. King wagged his tail and jumped up on her legs. He still had no idea what was going on, but he was beyond excited. Erin was his favorite person in the world, and he had never seen her this happy before.

"Ooooh! Ahhhh!" the other dogs barked. Cleo looked especially thrilled. She ran up and gave Erin a big lick on the cheek.

"Incredible," Cleo said. "Simply incredible. If this were an agility contest, I'd give Jin's maneuver a ten out of ten."

"What's happening? What is that thing?" King asked Cleo. "Is it a toy? Or is it a treat?"

"It's a *ring*, silly," Cleo replied.

"Oh, duh!" King said. But then he got confused. "So . . . does she chew on it or what?"

Jin was down on one knee now, holding Erin's hand, while King jumped up eagerly in between them. Jin was saying a lot of things to Erin, and King tried his best to listen.

"I love you so much, and I want us to spend the rest of our lives together," Jin said, looking lovingly into Erin's eyes. "I've wanted to ask you this for a few months, and I've just been waiting for the right time. Erin, will you marry me?"

"Yes! Yes! Are you kidding? Of course!" Erin wiped happy tears away from her eyes and gave Jin the biggest hug. She was laughing and crying at the same time. "I love you so much!"

"With my mom coming to visit next weekend, I thought, Wouldn't it be amazing if we were *engaged*? She can celebrate with us!" Jin said.

"That's perfect," Erin replied. Then she got quiet, like she was thinking. "Wait. What if . . . ?"

"What if what?" Jin asked.

"Let's get married next weekend!" Erin exclaimed.

"Oh, wow! That's so . . . soon!" Jin said, wiping his own eyes and laughing.

"While your mom is in town! We'll do something small while she's here. It'll be perfect! Why wait? I don't need a whole big thing—I just want to marry you!"

"Me too!"

"I can't believe I'm going to be your wife!" Erin said, smiling.

"I can't believe I'm going to be your husband!" Jin replied.

By now, all the other humans in the dog park were clapping and dabbing tears from their eyes. Some of them were filming and taking pictures on their phones. Even the dogs were getting emotional.

"Beautiful. Just beautiful," said a bichon on a nearby bench.

"Mazel tov to the happy couple," piped up a schnauzer from inside her owner's purse.

The other Good Dogs wagged their tails and panted happily.

"Wow! Amazing news," Hugo said. "Jin and Erin are getting married!"

"Nothing makes an old dog like me happier than seeing young love," Patches said. "I've been the dog of honor at more weddings than I can count on my paw. I once gave a toast—"

But King had too many questions to listen to one of Patches's stories. He ran over to Cleo, with Waffles and Petunia following him.

"What's a wife? What's a husband? What's a wedding?" King asked.

"What's a weekend?" Waffles added.

"What's going on?" Petunia asked. "I'm happy, but I don't know why."

"Erin and Jin are getting married," Cleo explained to the puppies. "It's when two humans decide to be partners forever. Like best friends."

"So, like me and Zoe!" Waffles yelped.

"Sort of," Cleo said kindly, then turned back to King. "It means our family just got a little bigger! Jin will probably move in with us. Maybe someday they'll have kids . . ."

King tuned out the rest of Cleo's sentence. He had just gotten used to his family and his home with Cleo and Erin. He had a lot of happy feelings about Jin, and had known him for as long as he'd known Erin, but . . . squeezing a new human into the house *full-time*?

The thought of this big change was scary to King. Jin came over three or four nights a week, and King felt that amount was perfectly fine, thank you very much. Plus, *kids*? His eyes wandered to a corner of the dog park where two toddlers were pulling on a Labrador's tail. *Kids seem . . . intense*, he thought.

"Congratulations, King!" Lulu's friendly bark snapped him out of it. "You must be so happy! Isn't this AMAZING? Isn't this the most WONDERFUL NEWS?"

"Sure," King muttered. He tried pawing at Erin's leg so she would pet him, but she was too busy giving Jin big smooches on the mouth. King whined and tried to convince himself that he should be happy, like Lulu said.

It's amazing . . . right?

CHAPTER 2

S IT, GIRL! AND roll over!"

Hugo watched as Zoe playfully shouted instructions at Waffles.

"I said, *sit. Down. Roll over!*"

But Waffles just stood, wagged her tail, and barked. Hugo was lying on the cool stone hearth near the fireplace in the living room while his puppy sister and human sister played on the carpet a few feet away. So far, Waffles had ignored every command Zoe tried.

"Sit," she tried again. "Waffles, I said sit!"

Waffles didn't sit. She stared at the bag of treats in Zoe's hand.

"Down."

Waffles didn't lie down. Instead, she ran in a circle.

"Close enough, I guess . . . Now roll over!"

Waffles stood up and started bouncing on her hind legs, trying to grab the treat out of Zoe's hands.

"Waffles! What're you doing?!" Zoe laughed. "You silly puppy!" She reached into the bag and gave Waffles a treat anyway.

Hugo sighed. He would have been shocked, except that it was the sixth time in a row this had happened. Waffles hadn't successfully rolled over once, but Zoe was rewarding her as if she were some kind of expert. Hugo had been lying nearby all afternoon, trying to look busy. He'd licked both paws, scratched his butt for a while, and chewed on his Fuzzy Bunny. Anyone paying attention would have thought, *Now, that's a dog with a full agenda!* But really, it was taking everything in him not to intervene in Waffles's "training."

Hugo was very modest and he didn't like to brag—but it was a simple *fact* that he was a master roller-overer. He had probably rolled over thousands of times. He could roll over to the left. He could roll over to the right. He could even do a little something he liked to call a "double roll-over," which is where he rolled over two times in a row.

He would get a little dizzy, but it made humans go absolutely wild. He was a golden retriever, but he liked to think of himself as a golden achiever because he was so accomplished. And so golden, obviously.

Hugo put his head down on his paws. Sadly, it had been quite a while since someone had asked him to roll over. Lately he'd been doing it when no one was home, just to stay in shape.

"Sit." Zoe was holding another treat over Waffles's eager eyes. "Roll over!"

Waffles playfully pawed at the treat, and Hugo suddenly decided he'd had enough.

Someone needs to teach this puppy how to roll, he thought. *And that someone is* this *someone.* He stood up, went over to them, and gently pushed Waffles out of the way so he could demonstrate a perfectly executed roll.

"Waffles, watch me carefully," he said. "See how I'm sitting? Now I'm lying down, pushing my front paws forward and sliding to the floor. Now I'm rolling onto my back, legs in the air. This is important. The belly is exposed here so the human may decide to give it rubs. Then I'm continuing the roll onto the other side, standing up, and, ever so subtly, taking a bow."

Hugo humbly bowed his head, ready for his treat. Zoe threw one on the floor, and he carefully ate it up.

"All right, all right, I get it," Waffles said impatiently, and she stepped in front of Hugo.

"Okay, Waffles, ready?" Zoe held out another treat for Waffles. "Roll over!"

Waffles tried to sit, lie down, and roll over, but Hugo could see on her face that she couldn't remember the order. She ended up doing everything all at once. *Splat!* She fell onto the floor, squirming around in a twisted-up mess. Zoe clapped her hands and gave her another treat.

Hugo rolled his eyes. Waffles was getting treats for doing nothing! That wasn't how it was supposed to work. Plus, how was she going to learn correct behavior if Zoe kept rewarding her like this? It was his job to intervene.

He ran back to his sisters and jumped between them, pushing Waffles out of the way. Whoops! He'd accidentally knocked over Zoe's bag of treats.

I'll apologize, he thought. *But first, I have a lesson to teach.*

He did another perfect rollover. Then he heard a loud CRUNCH. *Uh-oh.* He'd smushed the treats under his back. *But that's okay,* he figured. *A smushed treat is better than no treat at all.*

"See?" he asked Waffles. "See the *full* rotation? It's so important."

He stood up, staring at Zoe expectantly. But Zoe wasn't impressed by Hugo's rollover. In fact, she was glaring at him, her hands balled up in tight little fists on her hips. She looked *furious*.

"Hugo!" she shouted. Hugo was shocked by the anger and disappointment in her voice. "This is why I wanted a puppy! Because they're *fun*. You're no fun, and you ruined all the treats, so now no one can have them."

She scooped up what was left of the treats and stomped out of the room. Hugo was hurt. He liked having fun—*who didn't?*—but someone had to be responsible, especially with a new puppy in the house. In his experience, dogs couldn't be goofy *all* the time. Some dogs had to keep the lights on.

Oh yeah, the lights!

It was getting a little dark, so he ambled over to the floor lamp and turned it on with his paw, illuminating the bookshelf. *Much better,* he thought. He shook off the feeling that he'd disappointed Zoe and settled down in one of his favorite spots, facing the books. But wait a second—why was Neil Gaiman right next to Agatha Christie? He'd have to re-alphabetize the books soon. Humans could be so messy.

"Well, I guess I'll just go outside, then," said Waffles, sounding a bit down.

"I'll go with you," Hugo replied, not wanting Waffles to be left alone in the yard at night.

He quickly followed Waffles through the doggy door and into the backyard. He looked around. The yard was full of what Hugo thought of as "teachable moments." Everything from a ball to a swing was an opportunity to explain to Waffles the ways of the world. Most important, he thought, was teaching Waffles how to keep busy. *As the saying goes,* thought Hugo, *"Idle paws will get scratched up by a cat."*

"Hey, Waffles!" Hugo shouted. "There's a game I want to teach you. It's one of my favorites."

He led Waffles over to a hole in the fence where they could see the road.

"Here's how the game works," he explained. "You look through the hole, and you count the cars! Fun, right? I'll go first. Uh . . ."

The street was empty, so they sat in silence and waited. Finally, a car drove by.

"One. Isn't this fun?"

"What's the point of this game?" Waffles asked.

"To count the cars."

"But why?"

"If we don't count the cars, who will?" Hugo thought this was a perfectly acceptable explanation.

"But why do the cars need to be counted in the first place?"

"Because they do, Waffles."

"What if we chased them instead?!"

"Don't be ridiculous. We just need to count them. It, uh, it keeps the humans safe."

"But *how*?"

"I don't *know*! You're asking too many questions. Two, three!"

Waffles sighed a big puppy sigh. She clearly wasn't into the game. Suddenly, a familiar form came rambling along the sidewalk. A confident French bulldog, off his leash and all alone.

"Napoleon!" Waffles shouted through the hole. "It's us! We're in here!"

Hugo was getting along better with Napoleon lately, but he still felt wary, seeing the unpredictable dog by himself, away from his house.

"What're you doing out of your yard?" Hugo asked.

"You know me—I got bored," Napoleon answered, cool as ever. "Jumped the fence! Sometimes I like to have a short nighttime constitutional. Go for a stroll, find some sticks. Can't keep *me* contained. I'm wild. Like a wolf. But a wolf that's a dog."

Napoleon winked at Waffles, and Hugo scoffed. But he could tell Napoleon had ignited something in Waffles, because the puppy stood up and leaned her front legs on the fence.

"Can you teach me?" she asked Napoleon. "How to jump a fence?"

Hugo tried to change the subject. "So, ah," he said, awkwardly clearing his throat with a little bark. "How about that proposal this morning, huh? A wedding! Amazing, right?"

Napoleon and Waffles both just nodded.

Hugo kept grasping at sticks, so to speak. "Do you think we'll, um, you know, will we go to the park with Erin tomorrow?"

"Aw, gee," said Napoleon, mocking Hugo. "I wonder if we'll go to the park tomorrow, seeing as we go EVERY SINGLE DAY. Genius question, Hugo."

Hugo tried to think of a comeback but didn't have time. At that moment, the back door to the house swung open and Enrique walked outside in his soccer uniform, holding Hugo's leash. He ran over to Hugo with a big smile on his face.

"Hey there, buddy," he said, and gave Hugo some nice pets. "And what's up with you, little buddy?"

Enrique gave Waffles some pets too. Then he clipped the leash to Hugo's collar. It was time for their evening walk. Hugo happily let his tongue hang from his mouth.

Enrique had really stepped up to the plate lately, and was giving Hugo walks every single night. It was the best part of Hugo's day, by far.

But tonight he was hesitant to leave Waffles alone with Napoleon right outside the fence. It wasn't that he didn't *like* the bulldog. It's just that Napoleon could be a bad influence. After all, it had only been a month since he'd managed to persuade Hugo to be a bad dog for a day!

As Hugo followed Enrique out of the yard, he tried one last time to get Napoleon to leave Waffles alone and mind his own business.

"Hey, Napoleon, did you hear that a hamburger cart overturned down the block?" Hugo shouted through the fence.

"I'm not hungry," said Napoleon. "I already hit up the garbage outside of Luigi's Italian Eats on my way here. Ate a whole takeout container of day-old linguini."

"What are you looking at, buddy?" asked Enrique. "You see a squirrel or something?"

I wish, thought Hugo, taking one more look at Waffles and Napoleon before following Enrique out of the yard and onto the sidewalk.

It will all be fine, he thought. But he wasn't sure he believed it.

"OKAY, LULU," SAID Jasmine. "Sit up straight, girl, and listen carefully."

Lulu sat up and perked her ears. It was time for

♥ *Lulu*

another acting lesson, and Lulu didn't want to miss a single second.

"Today's lesson is Big Reactions," Jasmine explained. "You see, acting is all about *reacting*. And the bigger you can react, the better you'll be on camera. This is the most important thing you can learn, and you'd better learn fast, since you're about to be a big-time reality-TV star!"

Lulu thought Jasmine was exaggerating a little. She wasn't really going to be a "big-time reality-TV star," but she *was* about to be in a little segment for a YouTube series called *Workin' It! Professional Pups*. They were going to film Lulu for a couple of days to show how she managed her Instagram fame. The final piece would be only ten minutes long, but Jasmine was so excited that you'd have thought Lulu was about to be starring in a daily soap opera.

"Remember!" Jasmine said. "If this series goes well, you could get your own reality show on television. You never know, maybe someone important will see it and you'll get *discovered*! It might be a small YouTube show . . ."

But it could really take my career to the next level, Lulu thought, nodding along.

"But it could really take your career to the next level!" Jasmine finished. She had given this little speech several times before. "Now, time for some Big Reactions."

Lulu tried to act chill, but inside she was totally freaking out! Being on a YouTube show was going to be way different from being @LulusPerfectLife on Instagram, and she was definitely feeling the pressure.

On Instagram, Jasmine had all the control. She was able to choose the best pictures of Lulu and put filters on them to make sure her hair looked extra shiny. But the video series had its own team of editors who were going to choose *their* favorite footage, which meant that Lulu had to be perfect in every single shot to ensure that she'd be proud of the final product. Lulu knew a lot of dogs who had failed to make the transition from photos to video. MollieTheCollie. Mr. Chunk. What worked in a picture didn't always work in a *moving* picture.

"Okay, act *surprised*," directed Jasmine, and Lulu started jumping all around the room and spinning in circles. "Good girl! That was great!"

Oh, Jas, Lulu thought as she nuzzled into her favorite person's leg. *If only you could have seen me this morning when Erin got engaged! I did SUCH a good reaction!*

"Now act excited!" Jasmine directed. Lulu jumped all around the room and spun in circles again, but in more of an *excited* way. "Perfect, girl! Subtle difference, but I love it!"

Jasmine held out her palm with a T-R-E-A-T, and Lulu ate it up in one gulp.

"Good girl." Jasmine petted her head. "Remember, if

we make a big impression on these producers, you'll be the next huge star! Like Lil' Stinky!"

Wow, thought Lulu. Anyone who was anyone knew Lil' Stinky. He was a Cavalier King Charles spaniel who'd recently used his Insta fame to transition into a career as a rapper. He had just been featured barking in the background on Justin Bieber's new single, "Going for a Walk ft. Lil' Stinky," which was basically the song of the summer. Lulu didn't want to work in music—just TV, feature films, commercials, theater, and print modeling, with an international book tour and a line of best-selling calendars and key chains—but still, Lil' Stinky's level of success was inspiring.

She'd been learning a lot about acting in her daily lessons with Jasmine. Everything from emotional honesty to how to bark from her diaphragm to the importance of an up-to-date headshot. And now she knew all about Big Reactions!

A good dog is a good actor, she thought. *She listens, she tells the truth, she prepares. She takes care of her instrument.*

In Lulu's case, her "instrument" was her entire adorable self. She settled down on one of her many plush velvet pillows. Between witnessing a romantic proposal and another productive acting class, it had been a long day. As she closed her eyes, she imagined what life would be like after she and Jasmine became famous. Could @LulusPerfectLife get even more #perfect?

She saw a pink stretch limo with room for all of her friends from the neighborhood ...

A massive doghouse on the beach in Malibu, full of her favorite snacks ...

A paw on the Hollywood Walk of Fame ...

An infinity water bowl ...

Life is going to be pretty sweet, she thought as she drifted off to sleep.

CHAPTER 3

"MORNING, PATCHES! MORNING, Petunia!" King greeted his friends as they entered Good Dogs doggy day care.

"Wrestle?" Petunia asked him as she trotted into the living room.

"Sure thing!" King replied, sitting back and letting the pit bull pounce with the first tackle. It was the morning after the big proposal, and King was feeling a bit better than he had yesterday. Jin had stayed over the night before, and nothing major had changed for him and Cleo. They'd woken up, eaten breakfast, and had their usual morning run. Jin had even given him some T-R-E-A-T-S.

"How are you feeling about the wedding?" Petunia asked as they rolled around on the floor.

"I feel like maybe everything is going to be okay!"

King replied. When they were done wrestling, he sat by the door and greeted more of his friends while Erin talked to their humans above him.

"Morning, Hugo! Morning, Waffles!" King yelped.

"Morning, King!" Hugo and Waffles barked back in unison.

"Morning, Jasmine!" Erin said.

"Morning, Erin!" Lulu's owner, Jasmine, replied.

"Morning, everybody!" Lulu said, strutting in with her head and tail held high.

"So you're not even going to have a party?" Hugo's mom asked Erin. They were in the middle of talking about the wedding.

"Oh, no, we're just going to do a small thing at city hall," Erin replied.

"Well, we would *love* to celebrate with you two!" Hugo's mom replied. "You know, we could put something together in our backyard, if you want. Nothing too big, don't worry. Just a fun little party."

"Oh, I don't know . . . ," Erin started.

"Oh my gosh, it would be so fun!" Jasmine chimed in. "I'll help put it together! And if you need an officiant, I *am* a minister."

"Really? I thought you were an actress," Jin asked, walking in from the kitchen.

"I'm both," Jasmine replied. "I got ordained online.

And I'm also Lulu's social media manager, and occasionally a nanny, if you know anyone who's looking. And I yodel!"

"Let us throw you a wedding party! Next Saturday! It's the least we can do," Hugo's mom added. "After everything you do for the dogs."

King glanced up to see Jin and Erin sharing a look and smiling.

"Oh my gosh, we could get the dogs involved too! It would be hashtag fabulous," Jasmine said, excited. King didn't know her very well, but he totally understood why she and Lulu were best friends.

"You know, that *does* sound really nice," Erin said, turning to Jin. "Cleo could be the flower dog! And King could be our ring bearer."

Jin laughed. "Or swap those two. Do you really think we can trust the puppy with the rings? I almost thought the little goofball swallowed your engagement ring yesterday!"

Jin tried to pat King on the head, but King turned away.

Uh, yeah, but I didn't swallow the ring, bud, King wanted to tell him. *I did an awesome job and everybody loved it.* King couldn't believe Jin didn't trust him. Didn't Jin know he was the runner-up for "Most Improved"?

Then King got swooped up into Erin's arms and she gave him some really wonderful rubs on his chest.

"Awww, don't listen to him, King," she said playfully, then turned back to Jin. "We just have to show King what's expected of him. When he knows what to do, he's the sweetest little doggo on the planet."

Now, that's more like it, King thought, and he gave Erin her favorite: a big slobbery kiss on her face. And then she gave him his favorite: a bunch of tiny kisses all over his face. Jin watched their smoochfest, smiling, with his hands on his hips. King turned his head and made direct eye contact with Jin.

That's right, my guy, King thought. *You might be moving in, but nobody comes between an Erin and her King!*

Jin gave King a nice little scratch under the chin as Erin waved goodbye to Jasmine.

"So, it's decided, then?" Hugo's mom asked, still standing at the door. "A wedding party in our backyard, next Saturday? With all the dogs? Jasmine officiates?"

Erin looked at Jin, then at King and Cleo, and then back to Hugo's mom.

"Oh, why not? That sounds really lovely. Thank you!"

King didn't really know what any of that meant, but Lulu seemed especially excited.

"A wedding! How perfect!" she said dreamily. "If there are two things everyone loves on Instagram, it's dogs and weddings. And I'm about to be a dog *at* a wedding? It's too good to be true."

Hugo looked slightly more nervous. "If Erin and Jin are planning a wedding, and our owners are helping, we're all going to need to be on our best behavior all week," King heard him explaining to Waffles. "It's like the time Enrique had a big test coming up and I didn't distract him with a tennis ball for a whole two days. Except, like, a hundred times more important."

King spent the next couple of hours doing a handful of his favorite things. He played with his friends. He played with his squeaky toys. He peed in the yard. He smelled his pee. He tried for the millionth time to catch his tail in his mouth. Then it was time to head to the dog park and do all of the same things there.

"All right, everybody, line up!" Erin announced, grabbing their leashes. The good dogs excitedly gathered by the front door and sat patiently. "Let's get some fresh air— Wait, hold on."

Her phone was ringing in her pocket, and she put the leashes down on the counter to answer it.

"Hello? . . . Yes, this is she. May I ask . . . Oh. Wow! That's amazing."

King could hear only bits and pieces of what Erin was saying, but she sounded happy, so he inched closer to the kitchen to eavesdrop.

"When would it be? . . . Oh. And for how long? . . . Okay. And are there any other options, schedule-wise?"

Erin paused. King could see her feet nervously pacing. Then she sat down and said sadly into the phone, "I'm sorry, but I don't think I'll be able to make that work. Thanks, anyway."

Erin hung up her phone. King didn't know much about those strange little rectangles, but he knew that when they talked, people listened. Sometimes they made people happy; sometimes they made people sad. Right now, Erin looked sad. King rested his head on Erin's foot, curious about what the rectangle had said to make her upset.

"Who was that?" Jin asked, walking in from the living room, where he had been doing work on his larger rectangle. King knew that Jin's job was to use his fingers to make a *clack-clack-clack* noise on the rectangle. He was very good at it, and he was working from their house today.

"It was Champion Academy," Erin replied.

"Whoa! That agility training school? The one you said is the best in the whole state?"

"Yeah, that's the one. I applied months ago for Cleo," Erin started, and Cleo ran into the kitchen as soon as she heard her name. "And she got accepted off the wait list."

"That's amazing!" Jin said, and then patted Cleo on the head. "Congrats, Cleo! That's great news. So why do you look so upset?"

"Because I had to decline." Erin sighed. "The training session starts tomorrow, and the trainer needs to accompany the dog. I'd have to go with her. We have a wedding to plan, and with your mom coming to visit . . . not to mention, I can't close Good Dogs for that long!"

She got down on the ground and gave Cleo a big hug. "I'm sorry, girl," Erin said. "Maybe next year."

"No, call them back!" Jin insisted. "Tell them you can do it. I can work from home next week, which means I can run Good Dogs for a bit. No need to close down!"

Erin looked surprised. "Really?"

"Yeah! And I can deal with my mom and the wedding details. It's just a backyard barbecue around the corner, it'll be fine. I know how important this training school is to you. And to Cleo."

"Are you sure?" Erin asked, smiling.

"Look, if I'm moving in, I'm going to have to learn how to help out with Good Dogs at some point, right?" Jin asked. "Might as well start now."

"It's a lot of work," Erin said, gesturing to all of the dogs in the front hallway. Waffles was trying to climb onto Petunia's back. Lulu was barking loudly at the mirror. King had a feeling she was "practicing her act-ing" again—either that or she was just confused.

"So you'll teach me what I need to know," Jin said sweetly. "I promise they'll be fine."

Erin picked up King. "That okay with you, buddy? Spending a week with Jin?"

King was terrified. Jin was nice, but he didn't like the idea of spending all that time *without* Erin. But he didn't want to let Erin see he was scared, and plus, her face smelled so good. It smelled like . . . *face!* So he licked it again.

"All right, I'll call them back!" Erin said happily.

So it was decided. Erin and Cleo would be gone for a whole *week*. Jin was going to be in charge of Good Dogs for a whole *week*. And Jin and Erin were going to get married *next week*! King was nervous about so many things, but he knew one thing for sure: He was going to have to ask Hugo and Lulu how long a week was.

THAT NIGHT, AFTER a long day of playing in the park, the yard, and the house, King settled down in his doggy bed next to Cleo in their bedroom. But King was confused—it felt like they were going to sleep right after dinner, instead of cuddling on the couch with Erin like usual.

"What happened? Are we in trouble?" King asked Cleo.

"No, silly!" Cleo explained. "Erin and Jin just went out for dinner to celebrate their engagement!"

"Oh, okay," King said softly. But he didn't feel any better. He always got less attention and fewer snuggles when Erin was out of the house. King couldn't put his paw on it exactly, but it always felt like Erin was less "present" when she was gone. *Does getting married to Jin mean there will be more nights like this?*

"You must be excited about Champion Academy," King said, trying to take his mind off the anxiety.

"I am!" Cleo answered. "A whole week of agility training!" She kept talking, but King zoned out. The thought of Cleo being gone for a week, which he had learned was made up of seven whole trips to the park and roughly fourteen whole meals, made him even sadder. He whined.

I know what I'll do, King thought. I'll do what I do whenever I get sad at night in bed! I'll stare at the moon!

That ol' circle always knows how to make a pup feel better...

So he looked out the window, like he did every night—but something was different. There was a desk blocking the bottom of the window, so he couldn't see the moon!

"Nooooo!" King howled. Then he looked around the rest of the room. A lot of things were different! Jin had been moving his stuff in, and there were bags and boxes everywhere. King remembered that Erin had told them his and Cleo's room was soon going to double as Jin's home office.

Would Erin getting married mean he'd never be able to see the moon again? How was he supposed to go to sleep without the moon's calming presence in his life?

"Everything's changing, Cleo!" he barked. "And I don't like it! Will Erin even want us as part of her family when Jin moves in? He's going to be her new family!"

"Calm down," Cleo said, snuggling up next to him. "Change can be good! There's room in our family for the two of us *and* Jin. Duh!"

"Okay."

"Erin loves us. She made a commitment to us, and she'd never go back on that."

"Okay." King gulped. He tried to stop his paws from shaking and his stomach from feeling funny.

"Will you promise me that you won't freak out while I'm gone?"

King just rolled over on his back.

"King?" Cleo asked again. "Promise me. Erin and Jin have enough on their plate with the wedding. And you've been such a good dog lately! Promise me you'll be calm?"

"I promise," King said. "I'll be good. I'll be fine. I'll be good. I'm a very calm dog, you know?"

Cleo didn't need to say *really?* because that's what she was saying with her expression.

I'll be good. I'll be good. I'll be calm. I'll be calm. King repeated these mantras to himself as he tried to fall asleep, but as he tossed and turned without the moon's comforting presence, he wasn't so sure . . .

CHAPTER 4

Hugo

"YOU'RE SURE YOU'RE okay?" Erin's voice came out of Jin's phone as Hugo and Waffles walked in the front door.

They were the first ones at Good Dogs, aside from King, of course. It had been a few days since Erin and Cleo left for Champion Academy, and Hugo and Waffles had been first to arrive every morning. Hugo looked up at Jin and could see a tiny Erin inside the phone. Tiny Erin looked nervous.

"Everything's fine!" Jin said comfortingly. "I've gotten us through the last few days, haven't I?"

"But you've got a full house today. Napoleon and Lulu and everyone. Are you sure—?"

"I'll be all right," Jin replied. "I can handle it."

"Well, okay . . . if you're sure," she said uncertainly, and Jin nodded. Hugo gave a hearty bark up at the phone and wagged his tail confidently.

Not to worry, Erin, he wanted to tell her. *I've been extra responsible in your absence!* The truth was, Hugo had been helping out a lot, and Jin had been doing just fine so far without Erin around. Sure, things had been a little stressful, but no major emergencies, bark on wood.

On Monday, Petunia ate some cheese off a table, but Hugo got her to stop. On Tuesday, Jin got all the leashes tangled up on the way to the park, and Waffles ran off— but Hugo acted quickly and grabbed her leash in his mouth. Crisis averted. And yesterday, King knocked over the trash can a few times, but it was an honest mistake. All in all, Jin seemed sort of anxious, but he was trying his best, and Good Dogs was in good hands—and paws.

"Please don't worry about anything," Jin assured the tiny Erin in the phone. "We're totally fine here. See you tomorrow!"

Erin smiled, blew one big kiss to Jin and one to King, and hung up. King sulked toward the couch. Waffles must not have noticed that he wasn't feeling himself, because as soon as he got into the living room, she pounced on top of him for their usual morning wrestle. King seemed distracted, but Hugo knew he'd never pass up a wrestle.

"Careful!" Jin shouted at Waffles and King. "Hey, hey, down!"

Hugo shook his head. Jin *clearly* couldn't appreciate a good wrestle. Then the doorbell rang and Patches ambled in. Hugo walked over to him and sniffed him hello.

"Hello, old boy," Patches said. "New boss this week, huh? Reminds me of a story. Did I ever tell you about the time I found my owner's slipper under the couch? The year was 2015, and the world was a different place . . ."

Hugo curled up near the old sheepdog to listen. This was going to be a long one, he could tell.

"TikTok hadn't been invented yet, and a *fortnight* was simply the number of weeks it took to eat an entire bag of kibble," Patches continued. "Speaking of which, did I tell you about the time I ate an entire bag of kibble? The year was 2017, and the world . . ."

Thankfully, the doorbell rang again and Hugo had an excuse to get up and bark.

"Here we go," Hugo heard Jin mutter. "Another one!"

Then Petunia strutted in, as energetic as ever, and looked at Waffles and King. "Hey," she yipped. "You started without me! No fair! Now I don't know how the beginning of the wrestle went." She immediately leapt into the fray and turned the two-way wrestle into a three-way wrestle.

Jin tried to break them up again. "No, no," he said nervously. "Not inside. Please!"

Jin went to grab Petunia, but the doorbell rang again, and he walked back to let in Lulu. She waltzed in, sat in the corner, and got right down to business.

"Patches, Hugo, come!" Lulu commanded.

They both walked toward her.

"Sit."

They sat. Hugo didn't know what this was all about, but he loved to sit.

"Good boys. Now, I have an important question to ask you."

"I love questions," said Patches. "A question is merely an answer in reverse."

Lulu stared at Patches for a while. "Okay, moving on," she finally said. "My question is this: Which side is my good side?"

"Side of what?" Hugo asked.

"My face," Lulu replied. "This one, or this one." She slowly turned her face from side to side.

"I don't know if I could choose," answered Hugo. "Seems to me that you need both."

Lulu sighed. It was clear that was not the answer she was looking for. "Ugh, never mind," she said. "It's just . . . the YouTube crew is coming over *tomorrow* to take pictures before the big shoot! I need to prepare all my best angles."

Hugo was excited about his friend's big acting opportunity. He couldn't wait to watch the video when it came out, even though whenever his family showed him videos of other dogs, he had a tendency to get very confused and bark like a maniac.

"I need to practice," Lulu continued. "Wanna see some *acting*?"

Hugo and Patches both nodded. Across the room, Hugo noticed that Jin was holding a flailing Petunia in the air while Waffles jumped and yapped at his sneakers. King was running around wildly in tiny circles. Jasmine, who had just dropped off Lulu, was saying goodbye.

"So excited for the wedding this weekend!" Jasmine said. "Can't believe the rehearsal dinner is already tomorrow!"

Jin nodded politely, smiled, and waved goodbye, but as soon as she was gone, he started rubbing his head with his hands, looking incredibly stressed. Hugo considered intervening, but he actually *did* want to see some acting. He turned back to Lulu.

"So, Jas has been teaching me about Big Reactions. Watch. Patches, what day is it today?"

"Thursday," answered Patches. "Which reminds me. Did I ever tell you the story about the time I ate that calendar?"

"How *dare* you!" Lulu screamed, and she slapped Patches across the face with her front paw, making him yelp.

"Hey! Why'd you do that?" Patches howled.

"*Acting,*" answered Lulu, rolling over with flair. "Here, I can do another one. Hugo, what's your favorite toy?"

"I don't want to say," Hugo whined.

"Why not?" Lulu replied.

"Because you're going to slap me in the face!"

"Now, why on *earth* would you think that?"

"Because you just did it to Patches."

"Okay, *detective*. Come on, don't be a scaredy-dog. What's your favorite toy?"

Hugo didn't want to say, but he also didn't want to be a scaredy-dog. "Fine," he answered. "It's my Fuzzy Bunny."

Suddenly, Lulu turned onto her back and started howling and whimpering! Hugo had never seen her like this. She was acting like she'd been hit by a car or something! Jin put down Petunia, ran over, and scooped up Lulu.

"Hugo! Patches!" he shouted. "What did you do to poor Lulu?!"

Hugo gasped. He would never hurt a hair on Lulu's head, and the accusation was highly insulting. Didn't Jin know that he was a lover, not a fighter? And Patches had never hurt anybody in his whole life, except  for that poodle he'd bored to death with a story about the time he saw a bird. Well, he'd at least bored the poodle to sleep, and she didn't wake up for a *long time*. Either way, she never came back to Good Dogs after that.

Lulu stopped whimpering and licked Jin's face. Confused, he set her back down, saying, "I guess she's all right . . . That was strange."

"Hey!" Hugo barked at Lulu after Jin walked away. "Why'd you do that?"

"Acting," she said, perking her ears up. "Convincing, right? It's all about Big Reactions!"

Hugo didn't have time to come up with a response, because right at that moment the doorbell rang again and Jin ran over to answer it.

"Oh no," Jin muttered, and Hugo turned to see Napoleon standing in the doorway with his owner. Jin pasted on a smile and thanked Napoleon's owner, who then let Napoleon off his leash. The sturdy French bulldog ran straight toward King, Petunia, and Waffles, turning their three-way wrestle into a four-way wrestle.

Uh-oh, thought Hugo. *That's too big of a wrestle for this little room.*

And he was right. Out of nowhere, Petunia let out a yelp. "Ouch!" she cried in Napoleon's face. "That's my ear! You nipped my ear!"

Napoleon growled back and then started to bark, which startled King, who backed away from the skirmish and—SLAM!—bumped right into the coffee table.

"King, look out!" Hugo called, but it was too late. He watched as the table, which was covered in fifty or so plastic bottles decorated with teeny pink hand-painted flowers, jumped into the air and swayed side to side. All the bottles slid off, breaking open and coating the hardwood with a slick purple liquid. King had managed to jump out of the way without getting hurt, but now the floor was an absolute mess.

Jin took one look at the spilled bottles and let out the most complicated human swear word Hugo had ever heard.

"King, what are those bottles?" Hugo asked.

"I don't know." King gulped. "But I know they were for the wedding."

"Too many dogs," Jin murmured to himself as he headed toward the kitchen. Hugo saw King's ears and tail droop. Hugo walked toward his friend to cheer him up, but was stopped in his tracks when he saw that Waffles had sidled up next to the mess with her tongue out. She was cautiously tasting the mysterious liquid on the floor.

"Yum!" she said. "Hey, Napoleon, you should taste this purple stuff. It's sweet and a little spicy, and it came out of a beautiful bottle, like some kind of secret human treat!"

"Waffles, don't do that!" Hugo barked at her, but it was no use. Napoleon also tasted the liquid and agreed that it was delicious. Then all the dogs except for Hugo and Lulu began joyfully lapping up the strange gooey juice. Hugo gave Lulu a desperate look.

"I'm being very careful about what I eat and drink before my big shoot," she said.

Jin came back into the room holding a mop, but as soon as he saw the dogs drinking the liquid, he absolutely freaked out.

"No!" he practically screamed. "No, no, no, no, no!"

He ran over and started frantically cleaning up the liquid, pushing the dogs out of the way with the mop.

"Why's he so upset?" Petunia asked, licking her lips to devour even more of the purple stuff. "He's making me nervous. And when I get nervous, I get gassy. And when I get gassy, I get even more nervous. Sometimes it goes on like that all night."

Jin was pacing now, talking anxiously on the phone.

"And all the bubble liquid spilled on the floor! . . . Yeah, the bubbles for the end of the wedding. And that's not all. The dogs started licking it up . . ."

Then, without warning, Petunia let out a long, loud fart. As she did, a perfect, shiny soap bubble emerged from her rear end. Hugo could not believe his eyes. The dogs all stared in disbelief. Then there was a long, collective *whoooa*, as if the others were impressed by Petunia's trick. Jin watched in horror, his jaw hanging open, seemingly unable to move.

"Cool!" Waffles exclaimed. "I want to do that!"

Waffles concentrated for a moment and then farted out a shiny bubble of her own. King, Petunia, Napoleon, and Patches cheered for her, and before long, they were all farting up a bubble storm together and laughing hysterically. Lulu wasn't participating, but she was watching, amused.

"Hey! Check this out!" King barked. He farted a bubble, then spun around quick and popped it with his tongue. Hugo didn't think it was funny. Well, maybe it was a *little* bit funny. But it was immature, he told himself. And he was supposed to be the responsible one! And those bubbles were supposed to be for the wedding! He stepped into the middle of the fart bubble cloud and tried to put an end to the madness.

"Come on, everybody! Grow up," he said. But just then, Petunia stopped laughing and looked stunned. Her eyes widened, and in one quick motion she puked out a big, foamy, purplish mess onto the floor.

Waffles looked impressed.

"Whoa, you *made* that?!" she asked. "I want to make one too!"

Waffles started coughing, trying to make her own foamy mess, which eventually caused her to puke on the floor as well. At the sight of the puke, King started to gag, and then he puked too.

"I never puke," Patches said. "Got an iron stomach from eating so many sandals. But one time I did sneeze thirty-six times in a row. My owner said it was a new, umm, uh—"

Suddenly, Patches heaved and puked all over the floor, and it was the biggest puke of all the dogs. After staring at his own barf for a moment, he shook it off and regained his composure.

"Record," he finished.

Hugo looked at Jin, who was standing in the middle of the vomit-covered living room, holding his mop as bubbles of dog fart floated gently through the air. He looked about as miserable as Hugo had ever seen a human look.

"THEY'RE GOING TO be just fine."

Dr. Gopalan smiled as she led Hugo and Waffles into the lobby of her office. Their mom was waiting there, along with a downtrodden Jin. Around them, the owners of other Good Dogs were collecting their own dogs. Hugo had been to Dr. Gopalan for routine vet checkups, ear infections, and a weird rash, but he'd never gone to her office because of a bubble-farting incident. He wondered if *any* dog had ever been to the vet for that reason before.

"The soap bubbles weren't toxic," Dr. Gopalan explained to everyone in the waiting room. "They just didn't agree with the dogs is all. Their systems will sort things out naturally, but in the meantime, they shouldn't be fed until they've gone twenty-four hours without vomiting."

Jin sat with his head in his hands.

"I'm so, so sorry," he apologized to the humans. "Naturally, I will cover all the vet bills."

Hugo's mom put her hand on Jin's shoulder.

"Don't worry yourself," she said. "We have pet insurance, and anyway, this isn't your fault! Dogs can be unpredictable, and you have a lot on your plate right now. Tomorrow is another day!"

"Yeah, don't feel too bad," Jasmine agreed, picking up Lulu to leave. "And speaking of tomorrow, we've got a big photo shoot *and* the rehearsal dinner. Gotta take this little poof to get a haircut."

Hugo heaved a sigh of relief. If Jin wasn't in big trouble, maybe *they* wouldn't be in big trouble, either. But as he and Waffles walked to the car, their mom started to lecture them.

"You two really messed up today," she said. "What were you thinking?"

She sighed as she lifted them into the back seat, then started driving them home. "What am I gonna do with you?" she asked. "Well, I suspect you've punished yourselves enough. But you heard the doctor. No dinner tonight, and no breakfast! Hope you feel better before everyone comes over to our house tomorrow!"

No dinner?! No breakfast?! Hugo thought. *No fair!* He whined pathetically.

Mom looked at him in the rearview mirror. "Oh yeah? You shouldn't have eaten that bubble stuff, then!"

"But I didn't eat the bubble stuff!" Hugo tried to explain, but it was no use. He knew that she just heard a bunch of cranky barks. Hugo glared at Waffles, who quickly looked away.

"You're in big trouble," Hugo told her. "I know you're just a puppy, but this is ridiculous! You should have never started that whole bubble thing. You need to learn to be a good dog . . . *or else!*"

Waffles whimpered and curled up into a tiny ball. "Or else what?" she asked, clearly upset.

Hugo huffed. He hadn't really thought about an "or

else," but he was feeling really angry, so he said the first thing that popped into his head. "Or else it's back to the shelter!"

Waffles gasped. It looked like the wind had been knocked out of her, or like her fluffy brown fur had deflated. And Hugo immediately felt worse than he had felt in a long, long time. He spent the rest of the car ride overcome with regret.

What did I just do?

CHAPTER 5

*A*H, HOME, SWEET *home*, Lulu thought.

She wasn't actually anywhere near her home, but she figured it was close enough. She was sitting safely in her pink rhinestone carrier on the bus seat next to Jasmine, taking their usual bumpy ride through the city. She was glad to be back with her BFF after the chaos that morning at Good Dogs.

"I can't believe they ate all those bubbles, girl!" Jasmine said, patting her head through the top of the carrier. "I know you're too smart to get caught up in that wild behavior. No matter what Jin said."

Lulu looked up and tried to give a Big Reaction that said, "Yes! Exactly! I would *never!*" Was it too close to her surprised and happy reactions? She wasn't sure.

"No dog who had a shrimp-and-asparagus frittata for breakfast would be lapping up soapy bubble juice like it was champagne."

Lulu licked Jasmine's hand. She was so grateful to have a best friend who really *understood* her, beneath all the floofy fur. And speaking of that floofy fur—Lulu knew it was a bit floofier than usual. She needed a trim. They were on their way to the groomer so Lulu could get gorgeous for *Workin' It!* Lulu was excited and anxious at the same time. She was determined to make sure her big internet-video debut was a success. She wanted to show Jasmine how much she cared! And plus, if she became a big #star, maybe they could make enough money to afford a car and stop taking the bus.

The doors opened, and Jasmine carried Lulu off the bus. Lulu smelled all the familiar smells as they walked the few blocks toward GROÖM, her usual salon.

Hey, Lulu! Hi, Lulu! Wow, look! Lulu's back! Lookin' good, Lu!

Lulu imagined the various ways she'd be greeted by her friends and fans at the salon as they walked through the front doors and toward the receptionist's desk. Jasmine set Lulu's carrier down on the counter, and Lulu started to imagine her haircut.

A trim around the sides . . . short but not too short . . . a bow on top! Time to get glam for the cam!

But she was jolted from her daydream by Jasmine's disappointed voice. "Oh no. Really? Where's Lynn?"

"She's out for the week," the receptionist said. "Her sister is having a baby, and she's helping out!"

"Awww, that's nice of her," Jasmine replied. "But we always get Lulu's hair cut by Lynn."

Lulu couldn't believe it. Lynn wasn't available to cut her hair?! *Who allowed this to happen?*

"No! Not okay! I'm furious! Lynn must return!" Lulu exclaimed. So what if all the humans could hear were high-pitched yelps? They needed to know she was upset!

How selfish of my hairdresser! How selfish of my hairdresser's sister! How selfish of my hairdresser's sister's baby! Lulu couldn't stop fuming. *Nobody consulted me about the timing of this birth! Couldn't it wait until after my big video shoot and Erin's wedding?*

"Can't someone else go help that lady with the baby? Problem solved," Lulu barked.

"Don't worry," the receptionist said to Jasmine. "We have a substitute groomer filling in. Beverly."

Humans liked to call this job a *groomer*, but Lulu didn't understand why. She wasn't being groomed, she was being *dressed*. Because her hair *was* her clothes. Lulu was skeptical about trusting her style to anyone besides Lynn, but the receptionist tried to sound reassuring.

"Beverly will do a wonderful job. She just came out of retirement."

Lulu didn't know what *retirement* was, but she sure hoped it was a fancy school for doggy hairstylists.

"Hmm," Jasmine replied, patting Lulu's head hesitantly. "I guess we don't have much of a choice, do we?"

To say Lulu was nervous would be a massive understatement. She was terrified to trust something this important to a person she considered to be, in the nicest possible terms, a total rando. But before Lulu could jump from her crate and run out the door, a dry, raspy voice piped up behind her.

"Is that a dog? Or did a marshmallow stick its finger into a light socket?"

Um, excuse me?! Lulu thought. *Nobody talks about me that way! Plus, I know enough about T-R-E-A-T-S to know that marshmallows don't have fingers.*

She and Jasmine turned to see that the voice belonged to an older woman with a terrible haircut and thick, pointy glasses, who Lulu assumed must be Beverly. She was pursing her lips at Lulu in disdain. So Lulu tried to do the same thing right back at her—another Big Reaction she needed to practice.

As Jasmine carried Lulu toward a hairdressing station, she explained to Beverly the importance of this haircut.

"She's actually a celebrity on Instagram, and she's about to get her big break this week," Jasmine said. "They're taking promotional photos tomorrow, so she needs to look *perfect*. Like this!"

Lulu watched as Jasmine pulled up a photo on her

phone. One of Lulu's favorites—an Instagram post from last year where Lulu was in a pumpkin patch at sunset, framed by a pink sky and red leaves falling from a tree, with the caption "PUP-kin Patch #FallVibes." It had racked up over nine thousand likes, and Lulu's hair looked #absolutely #flawless. But Beverly just shrugged.

"I guess if you want pedestrian and basic, I can do something like that."

Lulu did *not* like this woman's attitude. From the look on Jasmine's face, it seemed like she didn't, either. But they had no choice. Lulu was in the hot seat now, and Beverly pulled out her scissors. Lulu assumed the rude comments would stop once Beverly started working, but she was wrong.

Snip! Snip!

"Is this what passes for a *dog* these days?"

Snip! Snip!

"You know, there are *some* problems a haircut *can't* solve."

Snip! Snip! Snip! Snip! As Beverly's comments got snarkier, Lulu got even more anxious.

"Whoever did her last haircut is an *amateur*. Did they use a pair of plastic children's scissors?"

"Okay, maybe we can just focus on the grooming?" Jasmine offered.

Snip! Snip!

"I can tell that someone isn't deep conditioning," Beverly muttered. "And that someone is this dog!"

Who is *this lady?!* Lulu thought. *She has some nerve!* Lulu couldn't put her finger on it, but there was something familiar about this woman's rude demeanor . . .

"There," Beverly said matter-of-factly, finally setting her tools down. "I suppose that's about as good as it gets."

Lulu and Jasmine both scoffed in unison, insulted. Then, out of the corner of her eye, Lulu noticed something—or someone—saunter out of a back room.

"Well, well, well . . . ," a familiar voice uttered. "If it isn't my least-favorite sentient piece of laundry fluff."

What was *she* doing here?

"Pickle the cat," Lulu replied, trying to sound confident. "Fancy seeing you here. But then again, I'm fancy seeing everyone."

Nice one, Lu, Lulu thought to herself. *Thanks, Lu!* she thought back.

It had been only a month since Lulu, King, and Hugo had saved Pickle from the shelter and helped her get back home. And Pickle had helped them that day too. It had seemed their relationship was turning a corner, but Pickle had quickly reverted to her normal self—always ready with a cutting insult or mean comment.

"Did my owner give you an adequate haircut?" Pickle asked. "I suppose anything is better than what you walked in here with."

"Your *owner*?" Lulu yelped. She looked up at Beverly. Then back at Pickle. Then at Beverly. Then at Pickle. It all started to make sense. Beverly was Pickle's owner!

Pickle was Beverly's cat! She should have realized it sooner. They did sort of look alike.

No wonder Beverly has such a bad attitude, Lulu thought. *She must have learned it from her cat.*

But she didn't stay to chat with Pickle. Jasmine was ready to hit the road, and so was Lulu. Jasmine quickly paid for the haircut, thanked everybody, and they left.

"I think it looks good, girl," Jasmine said reassuringly, patting Lulu's hair as they walked toward the bus stop. But could Lulu detect a wavering in her voice? She couldn't tell.

When they sat down on the bench, Lulu immediately turned to the reflective glass of the bus stop. After barking wildly for a moment at the dog who looked back—*Reflections! Those strange, strange things!*—she eventually settled down and got a good look at her haircut.

Was it a little bit . . . off? Were her bangs uneven? Were her paws always this fluffy while the rest of her legs were not? Was that lock of hair supposed to come so close to her eye?

Lulu had a sinking feeling. What if the haircut was off enough to get in the way of her big break?

Just then, she smelled two familiar smells and saw two familiar faces. It was King and Jin, walking in the direction of GROÖM. Jin was talking on his phone.

"Yes, we're doing salmon for the dinner tomorrow.

Lulu 🖤 67

Yeah, salmon. And a barbecue on Saturday for the wedding."

"Jin! King!" Jasmine waved to Jin, who wrapped up his call. They stopped for some friendly small talk.

"Yep, getting this guy a little pre-wedding haircut too," Jin said to Jasmine as King excitedly sniffed Lulu's butt to say hello.

Lulu, still preoccupied with her hair, wasn't in much of a mood to talk, not even to a good friend. But she sniffed him back, and as Jin and King walked off toward the hairdresser's, she called after King.

"Good luck in there," she said ominously before turning back to her reflection. "And be careful!"

CHAPTER 6

THE NEXT MORNING, King couldn't stop scratching his ear.

Scratch! Scratch! Scratch!

Usually, this activity ranked among King's favorites. It felt good! But today the itch was so strong that scratching brought him no joy. He was just irritated.

Where's all my hair? he thought as he scratched and scratched and scratched.

Last night, Jin had taken him to get groomed for the wedding, but they'd gone to a strange groomer. And the rude woman had cut the fur on his head *way* too short! Not to mention that he thought he saw Pickle the cat out of the corner of his eye. Maybe that was just his stressed-out mind playing tricks on him, but the haircut was bad enough! When it was over, Jin kept saying how "nice and neat" King looked, but it didn't help. He was practically bald!

King felt as though he was known for three things: his adventurous spirit, his fun-loving attitude, his inability to count, and his lustrous border collie hair! Now one of those was gone! He didn't know how many things that left him.

He sat on the couch, letting his tummy recover from yesterday's bubble feast and scratching his ear where that hair used to be.

Will scratching bring the hair back? King wondered, unsure. *Only one way to find out.*

So he scratched harder, until he heard Jin's car pull into the driveway. He climbed onto the edge of the couch to watch through the window.

Jin helped a woman out of the car and grabbed her suitcase from the trunk. King had never seen or smelled this woman before, but he had a hunch this was Jin's mom, because of the family resemblance. She looked just like Jin but older, and with shoulder-length gray hair. Plus, they were both wearing pants. King figured it was possible that all humans wore pants, but he wasn't positive about that.

The front door opened and shut, and Jin and his mom stood in the hallway. King slowly, cautiously approached them. Jin and his mom were talking in a language King didn't understand. But maybe he could learn it? He started to get excited. He was jealous of dogs whose families spoke multiple languages. Hugo and Waffles's family sometimes spoke Spanish, so they got to learn two words for *snack* and *walk*! Did that mean they got double the snacks and double the walks?

"Here, King!" Jin called for him to come closer. Then Jin started speaking more quickly to his mom and gesturing nicely to King. King even heard his name a few times. He was pretty sure he was being introduced to a new person, which was one of his favorite things! He sat down in front of them and bowed his head, just like Cleo had taught him.

Jin's mom leaned down and gave him a few nice pats on the head, and then they kept walking through the house.

"Tsk, tsk!" Jin's mom said, waving her finger toward some dog fur in the corner of the room. King didn't need to speak her language to know what that meant. *Tsk* was the universal human sound of disappointment.

"Tsk, tsk!" she said again, pointing at a small spot of dried-up purple bubble liquid. Then Jin started to explain, pointing all over the room, speaking quickly, and holding up an empty bottle of bubbles. King had a feeling that Jin was telling his mom about everything that had happened yesterday. He even gestured toward King a couple of times.

When Jin finished the story, his mom looked at King. "TSK!" she said. That was the loudest one yet.

But it wasn't my fault! King thought. *Well, it wasn't just my fault. There were definitely some other dogs involved.*

King tried to shake it off and get some rest in the corner near the window, under a really nice sunbeam. But Jin's mom immediately started searching in a nearby closet, pulling out a mop, a broom, a duster, and a vacuum. King could tell from Jin's facial expressions that he was probably telling his mom to sit down and relax. But she wouldn't! All she wanted to do was clean!

This woman is going to get along great with Cleo! King thought. Cleo was the neatest, most well-organized dog he knew.

Normally, upon seeing a vacuum cleaner, King would have done his usual routine—bark at it for ten straight minutes as loud as he could. After all, how else would the vacuum cleaner know he was there? But today he had to be on his best behavior. He should clean up the room!

I helped make the mess, I might as well try to help clean it up, he thought.

Then he thought, *Wow, who's a good boy? Me!*

So he trotted over toward Jin's mom and made a grab for the duster with his mouth. *Let me be of some assistance, ma'am.*

But Jin's mom yanked the duster away from him! She waved her finger disapprovingly.

Okay, maybe she wants to use the duster . . . I'll help with the mop!

So he tried to grab the mop, but that was the same way Jin's mom was walking, and she got her foot caught underneath King's body. She nearly tripped and fell over!

"Ow!" Jin's mom yelped. Jin helped her regain her balance, and King scurried out of the way. She started speaking very fast and very sternly with Jin.

Uh-oh, King thought. *I hope Jin explains that I was just trying to help.*

But it was too late. Jin's mom came straight for King. She grabbed him by the collar and led him to his bedroom. As soon as he was in there, he turned just in time to see Jin's mom leave and quickly shut the door. What was going on?!

King didn't have much time to wonder, because a few minutes later, the door opened again and Jin's mom threw in all of King's toys from the rest of the house. His squeaky ball. His bouncy ball. His bouncy, squeaky ball. His blankie! His chewy stick. His blue moose. His yellow goose. All of his bones. Once all of his belongings were in the room, the door shut again.

What's happening here? King thought. He wasn't even excited to play with his toys . . . not in these circumstances. *Am I being confined to my bedroom? No way! This is my house! Not Jin's mom's house!*

As he looked around the room, he started to wonder

if he could even call it his bedroom anymore. More and more of Jin's belongings had been moved in, and it was getting crowded. There was *stuff* everywhere. Books, boxes, some high-tech rectangles.

Okay, King, take a deep breath, he thought. *Let's just lie down in bed.*

He went over to his doggy bed but was shocked to see that one of Jin's new boxes was in the way! Half of the box was covering the corner of his bed!

Um . . . WHAT?! King wanted to bark as loud as he could. He was furious! *Who does Jin think he is? Coming in here with his boxes, and his mom, and his haircuts?!*

Speaking of which, King's left ear started itching again. Everything was going wrong. And he was hungry! Like, really, *really* hungry. He hadn't been allowed to eat dinner last night or breakfast this morning. His tummy grumbled, and he let out a howl, staring angrily at the box on his bed.

This isn't Jin's room! It's mine! Mine! Mine! Mine! King thought as he circled the small office frantically. *I was here first!*

King knew what he had to do. He didn't know why he hadn't thought of it sooner. He had been around the block—both figuratively *and* literally—many times, and he knew what dogs did around the block when they were in this situation.

Someone was trying to take away *his* territory. He

needed to claim it back. There was only one thing he *could* do.

It had been a while since King had peed indoors on purpose. Last Christmas, to be exact. Seeing a tree inside the house had really thrown him for a loop. But now everything was changing, and Jin had left him with no other choice.

He lifted his leg . . .

CHAPTER 7

LULU SAT AT the breakfast table, staring off into the distance.

"Lulu? You okay?" Jasmine asked as she set up her phone to take their usual morning Instagram photo.

The truth was, Lulu didn't know if she was okay. She had woken up a lot earlier than usual this morning after tossing and turning all night. Today was going to be a big day, and she was anxious.

"Let's finish up this photo," Jasmine said. "The crew will be here soon!"

Lulu's morning routine was usually the same: wake up, pee, breakfast, Instagram, watch the likes roll in, poop. But this morning, the *Working It!* crew was coming over to take promotional photos, so her routine was somewhat different: wake up, pee, stress out, pace around the house, stare out the window forever, nervous poop.

Jasmine knew Lulu hadn't eaten any bubbles yesterday, so Lulu was allowed to eat breakfast, but she didn't want to. Instead, Lulu just kept staring out the window, feeling very "in her feelings," as Jasmine would say. Jasmine snapped a photo, then looked to see how it came out.

"Wow, girl," she said. "You look like you're in a black-and-white French film. Very chic. I love it! I'm posting this one."

Lulu's tail wagged a little. Jasmine always knew how to cheer her up. But then . . .

"Hmm, that's odd," Jasmine said.

Lulu cocked her head to the side and nudged Jasmine's arm. *What's odd?*

"Oh, it's no big deal, girl," Jasmine replied. "It's just, well, your Insta likes are a little lower than usual."

Jasmine held out her phone to show Lulu her post from the night before—a shot of Lulu sitting on a lounge chair on the roof of Jasmine's building, watching the sunset next to a giant mocktail, with the caption "A Furrrr-fect Sunset." Lulu had gotten pretty decent at reading from looking at Instagram several times a day (and from posing for funny pictures with so many books, magazines, and takeout menus).

It was true: The likes *were* lower than usual. It made no sense. The photo composition was gorgeous, the sunset was magnificent, and the caption was *hilarious*.

Usually, getting fewer likes than usual on a photo wouldn't have bothered Lulu. After all, a good dog knows that self-worth cannot be derived from likes on social media! But in this moment, she couldn't help but think that there was a reason for the unpopularity. Only one thing had changed: The Haircut. It couldn't be a coincidence. Lulu suddenly felt very insecure. She wanted to curl up in a ball and sleep the day away, but there was too much to be done. Jasmine was busy checking things off a very long to-do list.

"Time to pick out an outfit, Lu!" Jasmine said, opening the door to Lulu's closet.

Maybe picking out something to wear will cheer me up, she thought. But as she looked at all her beautiful outfits and costumes and accessories, nothing seemed quite right. She tried on a few options, but they just made her feel worse. Her ballerina outfit made her hair look uneven, and even the sequined gown couldn't draw enough attention away from her head. And Lulu was becoming more and more convinced that the hair on her head—and everywhere else, for that matter—was the problem. She walked to the corner of the closet and pawed at her astronaut costume.

"This one?" asked Jasmine. "But the helmet covers your whole face and head! No one will be able to see how cute you are!"

Lulu whimpered. *Exactly,* she thought. Jasmine

Lulu 🤍 79

finally relented and put Lulu into her orange astronaut suit and white helmet.

"Okay, girl. But you're going to have to take off the helmet when the crew comes."

Lulu nodded, but she wasn't sure she wanted to take off the helmet. Not now, not ever! It had dark tinted plastic in the front so that nobody could see inside. She'd wear it for the rest of her life if she had to, or at least until her hair grew out.

A few minutes later, the doorbell rang, and Jasmine let in a surprisingly big group of people, all holding cameras and equipment. There was a director, a photographer, a videographer, an assistant, a lighting person, and a young woman whose job, it appeared, was to walk around the apartment and say things like "OMG, this chair is so cute! I can't!" and "Would you just look at this tiny dog collar! I can't!"

"Okay, girl, they're ready for you," Jasmine said after the crew had set up their camera and lights. "They want to get to know you and snap some pics! Let's just take your helmet off."

Jasmine reached for the helmet, and Lulu whimpered and turned her head away. Jasmine tried again.

"Come on, girl. They need to see your face!"

This time Lulu let out a full yip, which made Jasmine sigh. The director walked over to see what all the fuss was about. She was a tall woman wearing ripped-up jeans, an oversize sweater, and a beanie. She seemed *very* cool. Lulu couldn't let her see The Haircut. Instead, she ran away and hid under the kitchen table.

The cool woman frowned. "Hmm," she said, holding her chin. "I'm sorry, Jasmine, we really are such big fans, but if Lulu's not able to pose for photos, how will she be when we start filming?"

Jasmine covered for Lulu. "Oh, she'll be fine," Jasmine said confidently. "I think she's just feeling a tad under the weather. She ate something last night that didn't totally agree with her."

Lulu wished Jasmine hadn't made up something that implied Lulu was having weird poops, but she was grateful for the lie nonetheless. And she had to admit, she *was* having weird poops this morning from the stress, but that was another story.

The director started packing up her stuff, and the rest of the crew followed her lead.

"Not to worry," the director told her. "Hey, how about this—if Lulu needs a little confidence boost, why don't you make an appointment with this new pet groomer? Name's Valentina Sorrentino. She just moved here from Milan, and she's supposed to be fabulous. I know how much a good haircut can help a dog's self-esteem."

And a bad one can basically ruin their life! Lulu thought, burrowing her head into the carpet.

The director handed Jasmine a flyer. "If you make an appointment with Valentina, let us know," she continued. "We've been meaning to profile her too. We could go with you, bring our cameras, and do a whole feature on it. We could call it 'Lulu's New Look' or something. Could be great."

"That is such a good idea. You're a genius! I can't!" said the woman whose job was still unclear.

Jasmine nodded and looked over the flyer as the film crew headed out the door.

She's from Milan, Lulu repeated in her head. *That is a very fancy place!* In fact, hadn't someone mentioned Milan recently? *Yes!* She remembered. Lulu went to PetCon, the premiere conference for celebrity dogs, every year, and this year GucciThePoochie was raving about all the places she had traveled. She had said that Milan was the new Paris. And that Paris, interestingly enough, was the new London. And that London was the old Milan. It was a lot to keep track of, but one thing was clear: Lulu *had* to go to this new groomer. Now. She ran toward Jasmine and wriggled out of the helmet.

"*Now* you take the helmet off?" Jasmine said playfully. "After they leave, silly?"

Lulu pawed at the flyer.

"What is it?"

Lulu barked and pawed at the flyer again.

"You want to go to this groomer? Okay, girl. I'll call that nice director and we'll set a time."

Lulu barked louder and whined this time too.

"You want to go *now*? I don't know, girl. We don't

know anything about this place. It's probably pretty expensive, and I have to pay rent this week."

Lulu whimpered. She didn't want to stress Jasmine out, but she really needed this haircut. *My life depends on this,* Lulu thought. *Doesn't Jasmine realize that?*

"My life depends on this!" Lulu yelped, and then grabbed the flyer in her mouth. Jasmine must have been able to tell that Lulu wasn't kidding around, and she finally agreed.

"Okay, let's go," she said. "Whatever it costs, we'll take it out of your sponcon income this month."

Lulu yipped with joy.

As THEY WALKED toward the fancy groomer's salon, Lulu poked her head out of Jasmine's handbag and took in all the sights and smells. They rarely went to this part of downtown, as it was mostly fancy art galleries and restaurants where the entrées were *very* expensive and *very* small. Lulu already felt fancier just being in the neighborhood. When they arrived at the address, there was just a bored-looking man sitting at a front desk. Lulu watched as Jasmine double-checked the flyer.

"Yeah . . . I guess this is it," Jasmine said with a shrug.

Typically, Lulu would be suspicious of an empty

waiting area, but the video crew had said this place was supposed to be chic, and big crowds didn't feel chic. So maybe it was a good sign that there was no one there.

Jasmine approached the front desk, and the bored man signed Lulu in without even looking up. He said Valentina would be with them shortly, and sure enough, a minute later an artsy-looking woman stepped out into the waiting room. She had giant tortoiseshell glasses and hair sticking out every which way. She was wearing a white button-down with paint splatters on it. Lulu knew this must be Valentina, and she wondered what part of her grooming technique involved paint.

"*Buongiorno,*" she said, and started slowly circling Lulu, occasionally muttering *hmm*, pointing at various parts of Lulu's body, and closing her eyes to think. "Interesting. Verrrry interesting. Yes. I think I can make my art on this canvas. Follow me, *per favore.*"

She spun briskly on her heels, and Lulu and Jasmine followed her into a back room.

Valentina lifted Lulu and placed her on a grooming table, facing a mirror. When Lulu finished her usual mirror barks, Valentina stood behind her and talked to her reflection.

"Right now you are a dog," she said. "When I am through, you will be a living, breathing, barking piece of art. You will belong in a museum. Let us get to work."

She then turned Lulu around so she could no

longer see herself, and got to work. Valentina used scissors, razors, brushes, and tools Lulu had never seen or felt before. Things were happening quickly all over her body, and it was hard to keep up. There was paint, glitter, and something that looked like mud but smelled a lot worse.

Lulu noticed that Jasmine's face was starting to fall a bit. She looked unsure.

Well, Jasmine's not as much of a risk taker as I am, Lulu thought, and felt better. As much as she loved Jasmine, Lulu always knew she was the real visionary of the duo.

"*Finito*," said Valentina. "I cannot believe. This is my finest work yet."

She spun Lulu around so she could look in the mirror, and Lulu found herself staring into the eyes of a dog she did not recognize. Sure, Lulu *never* recognized herself in mirrors at first, but this time was different. In fact, the creature staring back at her barely even looked like a dog.

The hair on her body was almost gone, and there were stars shaved in a random pattern. The hair that *was* still on her head was sticking up wildly in every direction and had been dyed *blue*! She raised her tail and was shocked to see that it was caked in sparkly glitter. The hair on her paws had teeny, tiny braids, and what were those jangly things under her chin? Were those *beads*? Lulu looked, and felt, like she had tragically collided with a crafts store.

♥. Lulu

Jasmine was speechless and had a shocked look on her face.

As they walked away from Valentina's salon, Jasmine finally spoke. "Girl, I hate to say it, but you kind of look like Albert Einstein."

Lulu didn't know who that was, but she assumed it was a very, very weird-looking dog.

Oh no, Lulu thought. *I had a bad haircut before, but now I have the worst haircut ever!*

Lulu 🤍

Hugo

HUGO SAT ON the top of the steps with his head on his paws. He watched as Waffles played with Zoe in the living room below. Waffles had been ignoring him all day, but he was determined to make things up to her. So he took a deep breath, grabbed a tennis ball, and slowly walked down the stairs toward them.

"Hey, Waff," he said, nudging the ball with his nose and rolling it in the puppy's direction. But she didn't even look up. She just kept getting belly rubs from Zoe. So Hugo grabbed Squishy Dino, one of Waffles's favorite toys, and dropped it at her feet.

"Want to play tug-of-war?" he asked. But Waffles just turned over, away from him. Hugo knew exactly why Waffles was upset, and he felt terrible.

"Listen, again, I'm really sorry about what I said yesterday, about the shelter . . . ," Hugo started. But Waffles got up and followed Zoe out of the room.

Hugo loved his new sister and wanted to make it up to her. But nothing was working. Last night he had given her his late-night treat, offered her unlimited playtime with *his* Fuzzy Bunny, and even lent her his special blanket to lie down on. He had apologized every chance he got. But nothing worked. She was spending all of her time with Zoe and ignoring him completely. And deep down, he understood. He had overreacted and said something that he didn't mean. He needed to be easier on her and not get so mad when she acted out. He needed to remind her that he could be fun!

"Kids! Put on your shoes! Time to go!" Mom called out from the kitchen. Sofia and Enrique ran downstairs as Dad helped Zoe put on her jacket.

That's right! Hugo remembered. *Everyone's going to run errands for the party tonight!*

The rehearsal dinner for Erin and Jin's wedding was later, and the kids were going to help Mom and Dad pick out some snacks and decorations. Hugo brought Enrique his shoes, then turned his attention back to the puppy. He trotted over to the front hallway, where his fluffy, poofy little sister was sitting at Zoe's feet.

I'll have some alone time with Waffles. We'll have fun!

"Hugo and Waffles, we'll be back in a couple hours!" Mom said. And then they were out the door. Hugo sat down next to Waffles, and they looked out the window to the street.

"All right, bud! Just the two of us," Hugo said excitedly. "Let's do something fun!"

Waffles didn't respond.

"You probably forgot how fun I am, since you've been spending so much time with Zoe. Sure, she's really fun. But who do you think she learned it from?"

Waffles didn't respond.

"Me! She learned it from me. Ol' Hugo's the king of fun. Any game you want! Wrestling? Racing? We could count cars again?"

Hugo thought he saw Waffles's tail wag just a touch, but he wasn't sure.

"Okay! Counting cars it is," he said, and he sat down next to her to look out the same window. "One, two, *three*—just kidding, that one was a mailbox! I'm being silly. Remember how silly and funny I am?"

The truth was, Hugo didn't really think the mailbox joke was *that* funny; it was just the first thing that came into his head.

"This is kind of boring," Waffles said softly.

Hugo smiled. At least she responded! "Okay, we can do something else," he replied.

"We could escape and go downtown!" she yelped.

"Um . . . what?"

"Napoleon told me he was going to jump his fence and go downtown," Waffles explained. "Do you remember how to open the gate in the yard?"

"Well, yeah," Hugo said. "It's not easy, you have to use the broomstick, but anyway—absolutely not!!!"

Hugo wasn't angry with Waffles, but he *was* angry with Napoleon for filling her head with ideas like that. And right before the wedding?!

"We're supposed to be good dogs this weekend," he continued. "Remember? We need to be on our best behavior! We can have plenty of fun right here without running away."

"Okay," Waffles agreed hesitantly. "I guess so."

They settled down again in front of the window and counted cars.

"Three, four," Hugo counted.

"Five, six," Waffles counted.

Hugo relaxed a bit, now that Waffles was on board for this very, very fun game. After a few minutes of counting, the clouds outside shifted, creating a really wonderful sunbeam that shone right through the window and made Hugo's fur feel warm and cozy . . .

"Seven . . ."

What a nice afternoon, Hugo thought. *Always nice to sit by the . . .*

His own inner monologue trailed off as he closed his eyes.

HUGO SLOWLY OPENED his eyes. He didn't remember falling asleep, but he knew that was how all the best naps started.

"Sorry, Waffles, guess I needed a little snooze . . . Waffles?" Hugo turned to see that Waffles wasn't sitting next to him anymore. He got up and looked around the house.

"Waffles? Where are you? I guess you win at counting cars."

But she wasn't in the living room or the kitchen. And he couldn't smell her, either. He barked upstairs but got no response.

Where is she?

He quickly ran out the doggy door into the backyard. Based on the sun's spot in the sky, Hugo guessed he'd been asleep for an hour or so. He turned to the gate and gasped in shock! It was open, and the broomstick was leaning against it.

Uh-oh.

Hugo

CHAPTER 8

U H-OH, KING THOUGHT for what felt like the millionth time today. *Uh-oh. Uh-oh. Uh-oh.*

He was in the laundry room now, surrounded by the small, circular fence. It had been about an hour since . . . The Incident. The Pee-Pee Incident. The Occurrence of the Indoor Pee. King wasn't sure what to call it, but he knew he shouldn't have done it. Getting confined to his bedroom with all of his toys was bad, but getting put in the laundry room with *none* of his toys was even worse. King knew he was in time-out, and he knew he deserved it.

Suddenly, there was a scratch on the window screen.

"Psst! Hey! It's me!"

King turned to see Hugo outside the window, standing on the air conditioner and whispering through the screen.

Uh-oh, King thought again. While he was thrilled to see his friend, he remembered that the last time Hugo showed up outside the laundry room window, it had led to a pretty wild adventure, and King wasn't sure he was in the mood for one of those. Plus, Hugo didn't seem like the type to sneak away from home alone. *Something strange must be going on.*

"Hey, Hugo," King whined.

"I need your help!" Hugo began, but then he changed his tone. "Wait—what happened to your fur? Did you get too close to the lawn mower again?"

"This is my wedding haircut," King replied. "Do you know how to make hair grow back? And also, what are you doing here?"

"It's Waffles," Hugo said, with concern growing in his voice. "She's gone! I don't know where she went, and I'm worried."

Hugo stopped talking suddenly and shook his head. "Wait, why are you in here again?" he asked King. "Are you in trouble?"

King took a deep breath and told his friend the truth. "Yeah. I sorta, kinda, maybe . . . definitely peed on Jin's tablet. You know, the rectangle that lights up—"

"What?!" Hugo asked, shocked.

"I know, I know. It was wrong," King replied. "I just

got so mad, and it seemed like the best idea at the time. I wanted to claim my territory. He had a box of stuff on my doggy bed! I didn't see the tablet. I just let loose with a big, powerful stream of pee-pee. I was peeing like a champ, all over the—"

"Okay, okay, I get it," Hugo interrupted.

"I shouldn't have done it, I know. I should have asked myself, 'How would I feel if *Jin* peed on my toys?' Well, I guess I *might* have liked that . . . I'm always interested in a new smell—"

"King, please," Hugo said. "We have a more pressing issue here. Waffles is gone!"

"Right, of course," King said. He felt nervous about Waffles. What if she was in danger? Hugo was the most responsible dog King knew. He wouldn't sneak away unless he was really worried, so this made King even more worried!

"I'll help you break out of here," Hugo said. "And we'll go find her."

"Oh, I don't know," King said. "I'm already in such big trouble."

"Exactly! You're already in trouble. How much worse could it get? Waffles needs our help!"

Hugo made a good point, King thought. How much worse *could* it get? He didn't have much to lose, all cooped up in the laundry room for the rest of the day.

And Waffles was his friend! He felt a special kinship with her. Mere months ago, *he* was a goofball puppy, just like her. Now he figured he was more of a goofball young adult, but he still had plenty of puppy tendencies.

Usually all my friends are worrying about me, King thought. Finally, he had an opportunity to be the mature one and offer to help. *After all,* he remembered, *good dogs help their friends.*

"Okay!" King said, determined. "Let's do this."

Getting the window open was a bit harder without Lulu's help, but after a few minutes, Hugo managed to nudge it with his nose and create an opening wide enough for King.

"Here goes nothing," King said, taking a few steps back so he could get a running start.

"You've got this!" Hugo encouraged him. "Just like last time."

King readied himself, then took off as fast as he could, leaping over the fence, then hopping onto a chair and out the window. King collided with Hugo, and they both tumbled off the air conditioner and onto the grass below.

"Ouch!"

"Oww!"

"Wow!" King exclaimed. "If there was an agility

contest for escaping from the laundry room, we'd get first place."

When they both regained their footing, King took some sniffs around the yard. "Ahh, do you smell that?" he asked Hugo, who shrugged. "Freedom! And also some of my bubble barf from last night. It's over there."

They sprinted away from the house and down the street.

"First stop, Lulu's," Hugo said. "She's the smartest of all of us. She'll know how to help!"

When they got to Lulu's house, King followed Hugo to the side gate that led to her backyard. Hugo pushed it open easily with his paw. Then they snuck onto Lulu's back porch and peered into her house through a window.

"What are you guys doing here?" came Lulu's high-pitched voice, but she sounded sadder than usual. King could hear her through the doggy door, but he couldn't see her anywhere.

"We'll get to that in a second. Where are you?" Hugo asked.

"Down here."

They looked through the doggy door flap to see Lulu sitting underneath her couch, all the way across the living room. Most of her body was blocked by a blanket hanging off the couch, so King could only see her paws and part of her tail. Was that glitter?

"I'm, uhhh, sick," Lulu said. "Yeah. I'm sick!"

"Well, we need your help!" King barked. "Waffles is missing, and we're going to look for her!"

"She said that Napoleon was going downtown," Hugo added. "Maybe she went with him?"

"Downtown? That's all the way downtown!" Lulu said. "I just got back from there. Long way to go for a puppy."

"We know! Will you help us?" King asked.

Lulu retreated farther under the couch and into the darkness. "I'm sorry, I can't," she said. "It's . . . uhhh . . . pneumonia. Yeah. Pneumonia."

"I didn't know dogs could get pneumonia," Hugo replied.

"I don't know what pneumonia is," King said. Maybe it was a sickness that gave you a glittery tail?

"Neither do I, but it's really bad!" Lulu barked. "It's contagious, it has nothing to do with my haircut, and I might even have to miss the wedding this weekend!"

"Oh no!" King exclaimed. "Feel better!"

As they walked away, Hugo could have sworn he heard Lulu whimpering inside. Strange—that wasn't like her at all.

"Huh. Must be the pneumonia," he said.

If Lulu isn't going to help, King wondered, *how are we going to find Waffles?* Then he had an idea, and he wagged his tail with surprise! He wasn't usually the one to come up with ideas, and it felt like digging in the mud and coming across an unexpected shiny rock.

"Let's find Napoleon!" King said to Hugo. "Maybe they're together? Maybe she followed him?"

Hugo agreed, and so it was a plan. They made their way carefully through the neighborhood on their way to Napoleon's house, ducking behind trash cans and parked cars anytime a person walked or drove by. The last thing they wanted was for someone to alert their people that they were running around off leash.

"He's probably not home," Hugo said as they walked up Napoleon's driveway. "But we should check just in case."

As they got closer to the house, they realized that neither of them had ever been farther than Napoleon's front yard, and they didn't know how to find him.

"I know," King said confidently. "Let's ring the door-bell." *Another good idea!*

Hugo just gave him a very skeptical look.

"What?" King asked. "I always run to the front door when I hear the bell! Maybe Napoleon will too! I bet if you stood on your—"

"Somebody out there?"

King was interrupted by the sound of Napoleon's voice booming from the backyard.

"Coming over for a surprise playdate?" Napoleon barked. "I'm around back! Hop onto that tree stump to jump the fence."

King turned to Hugo. "Too bad," he said. "I really wanted to ring that doorbell."

"Maybe next time," Hugo replied, and they walked toward the backyard. Hugo used the tree stump to eas-ily jump the fence, and then King did the same. What he saw when he landed was not at all what King had expected. Napoleon was lounging in a bright orange inflatable kiddie pool. He looked like he was on vacation.

"What?" Napoleon asked, sensing their surprise. "I like to sunbathe! And water bathe too."

Napoleon splashed some water onto himself and shook it off, getting King and Hugo a little wet.

"So, what brings you to my backyard?" Napoleon asked, rolling onto his back with his belly up.

"It's about Waffles," Hugo said. "She ran away, and we're trying to find her."

"I don't know anything about that," Napoleon replied.

"Really?" Hugo asked, unconvinced. "Because she told me that *you* said you were going to jump your fence and go downtown."

"Did you tell her that?" King asked. "Come on, Napoleon! You don't want her to get lost, do you?"

"Okay, okay," Napoleon said. "I may have mentioned *something* about going downtown. I wasn't really gonna do it, though. Sometimes I exaggerate for the kid."

"What else did you say?" Hugo asked.

"Not much. I just told her the story of the day we met her again. She loves that story. How we ran all over the Chic Patisserie and ate pastries out of the dumpster. Which, by the way, we should do again sometime! Maybe we could pencil that in for next Tues . . ." But Napoleon trailed off when he noticed King and Hugo's concerned looks. "I doubt she . . . ," Napoleon started. "Do you think—?"

"Thanks, Napoleon," King said. "Let's go, Hugo. We've got a puppy to find!"

"I'd join you," Napoleon offered, "but Finn gets home soon. Kid's been keepin' a pretty close eye on me these days."

King nodded and turned to leave the way they came in—there was a patio chair they could hop on to get over the fence—but Hugo turned around and got up in Napoleon's face.

"You better stop telling Waffles tall tales," Hugo growled. "You're a *bad influence!*"

Napoleon looked flattered. "Really? You think so? Thank you!"

"I'm not kidding, Napoleon," Hugo said. King

thought that Hugo really looked hurt. Napoleon must have thought so too, because his voice got a lot softer.

"You're right, I'm sorry," Napoleon muttered. "Telling stories like that makes me feel . . . cool, I guess. Won't happen again."

"Thanks," Hugo replied. "Lick on it?"

"Yeah. Lick on it."

Hugo and Napoleon licked each other's faces, and King nodded goodbye to the Frenchie in the pool. Hugo and King hopped over the fence and walked away from the house.

They trotted through their neighborhood, then through the next neighborhood, and another, until the buildings got closer together and the streets got more crowded. It was the same route they had taken to get downtown on the now-infamous bad day. People, dogs, cars, bikes . . . if he'd had time to sniff it all, he would have. But instead, King just followed Hugo's lead, moving stealthily to avoid being noticed.

Just two independent dogs going for a walk in the big city, King thought. *Nothing to see here. If anyone asks, we'll say we're going to work!*

"This way, I think," Hugo said. He was sniffing really hard now, following a familiar scent. King could smell it too, the unmistakable whiff of—

104   KING

"Pastries!" King exclaimed as they turned a corner and came face-to-face with the alley behind the Chic Patisserie. King was flooded with memories—some scary, but most of them really, really fun. He fought the urge to run right into the back entrance and eat everything in the kitchen. He remembered that he and Hugo were on an important mission.

King led the way down the alley, and they stopped in their tracks next to one of the dumpsters when they heard a familiar whimper.

"Hello? Anybody?" a voice whined from inside the dumpster. "Oh boy, I really messed up, huh?"

"Waffles? Is that you?" Hugo barked, his tail wagging every which way.

"Hugo?!" Waffles barked back. King couldn't see, but he imagined her tail, or entire body, was wiggling happily too. "I'm in here! In the big food bowl full of treats! I think I'm stuck."

"It's called a dumpster, remember?" Hugo explained. "Don't worry. We're gonna get you out of there."

Hugo jumped into the dumpster. King jumped in right behind him, landed comfortably on a wet, gooey trash bag, and immediately got a ton of sugar all over his paws. He looked up to see that there was some-how a banana peel on his head. Everything was sticky and smelled amazing. Waffles was in the corner, her fur coated in crumbs and icing. King didn't know how she had managed to get food all over her body, and he was kind of impressed.

"Let's get you out of here!" Hugo said to his little sister.

"Yeah!" King agreed. And then his eyes landed on a half-finished box of vanilla cupcakes. His tummy grumbled again. "Or . . . I don't know . . . maybe we could stay in here just a few more minutes?"

"We don't have time," Hugo said, and King nodded. He and Hugo helped push Waffles up over the edge of the dumpster, and she jumped down to the ground safely. King grabbed a piece of a raspberry scone for the road and jumped out of the dumpster to join her. Hugo followed behind them.

"You okay?" King asked Waffles. But she just looked down at the ground. King knew the expression on her face, because he made it all the time. She must have felt guilty and embarrassed to have gotten into trouble.

But before he could say anything to make her feel better, the back door of the bakery swung open and an employee spotted them.

"Dogs! Dogs! Those weird dogs are back!"

Hey! Who's he calling weird? King thought. He quickly scarfed down the rest of the scone and sprinted out of the alley behind Hugo and Waffles. They ran as fast as they could through the narrow city streets, until the houses started to spread out and they eventually recognized some lawns. They slowed down a bit and started to catch their breath.

"Phew. I bet if there an agility contest for jumping into dumpsters and escaping from an angry baker . . . ," King started, but Hugo wasn't listening. His friend was busy talking to Waffles.

"What were you thinking, running away like that?" Hugo asked her. "I was worried sick!"

"I'm sorry," Waffles said softly. She was walking with her tail drooping between her legs.

"You could have gotten lost! You can't act out like that again!" Hugo was getting really worked up.

"Come on, buddy," King said, trying to get in between them. "Go easy on Waff. She's a puppy! Puppies do silly things sometimes"—he smirked to himself—"or so I hear."

Waffles looked at King and wagged her tail a little, but when she caught Hugo's eye, she dropped it and looked down at the ground.

When they got back to Hugo and Waffles's house, King sniffed both of their butts goodbye and walked the rest of the way home by himself. It was getting late now, and the sky was a little bit darker.

He snuck around the side of the house and hopped up onto the air conditioner. The window was still open from his escape, and he figured he'd have no problem getting into the laundry room unnoticed. Jin had been so busy with the wedding planning, after all. He probably hadn't even noticed King was gone.

Great job, King! he thought. *You bravely rescued a friend, had a thrilling adventure, and got back in time for dinner!*

He hopped through the window opening and started walking toward his fenced enclosure, but suddenly there were two feet in front of him. Human feet! Jin's feet!

Uh-oh.

Jin was in the laundry room, waiting for him. Who knew how long he'd been waiting? Who knew how worried he'd been? King curled up at Jin's feet, ashamed. He felt exactly like how Waffles had looked a few minutes ago. King had thought he had nothing to lose by escaping with Hugo, but now he knew he must have been wrong.

Jin sat down on the floor next to King, and he *didn't* look happy. He looked stressed, and tired, and very relieved to see King, but still . . .

"Look, I know it's been hard without Erin," Jin said. "But you have to get it together while my mom is here, King! You can't just run away and come back all filthy!"

King wished he could explain *why* he had run away and come back all filthy. He thought if Jin knew it was to rescue a friend, he might be more lenient. "I only left so that I could help Waffles!" King tried to explain, but Jin didn't get it.

"Don't bark at me," Jin replied. "This is serious!"

Humans are such fascinating creatures, King thought. *They know so much and yet so little! They understand* when we're hungry, when we need a belly rub, and when we want to go outside, and yet they don't understand when we're going on an adventure to rescue our puppy friend from a bakery dumpster. Oh well! He buried his face in his paws.

"Listen," Jin continued. "No more running away, buddy. Okay? And no more peeing in the house. I have to get my tablet fixed now, on top of everything else. Do you know how hard it is to plan a wedding?"

King had never planned a wedding (*Maybe someday!* he thought), but Erin often left reality shows playing on TV for him when she left the house, so he had a pretty good idea of how stressful it could be. He nuzzled into Jin's leg and gave him a kindhearted look, as if to say, *I get it.* He really felt sorry for the way he had behaved today, and he wanted Jin to know it. So he curled up on Jin's lap.

Jin petted King on the head and gave him a little rub under his chin. "It's okay, buddy. All right, let's go."

Wait, what? Go? Go where? King wondered.

Jin stood up, and King realized he was holding a bag full of King's things. His blanket, his toys, everything. Then Jin's arm swooped down, and he picked up King too! Jin carried him out of the room, toward the garage door . . .

Whoa, whoa! What's going on here?

CHAPTER 9

LULU WAS LYING on the floor of her closet. Aside from one brief stint hiding underneath the couch, she had been there since they got home from Valentina's salon.

"I actually think it looks kind of cool," Jasmine said from the other side of the door. She'd been trying to cheer Lulu up all day, but to no avail. "It's very, um . . . smart! It looks like fireworks bursting in the sky!"

Despite Jasmine's best efforts, Lulu thought she didn't sound very convincing.

"I know what will cheer you up! An Insta post. Come on!"

Lulu just huffed and buried her head under one of Jasmine's shirts on the floor. This was a *disaster*. There was no way she was going to be on *Workin' It!* now. She would just hide in her closet until the crew forgot about her and moved on to some more deserving dog with a better haircut.

"No? Okay, girl," Jasmine said as she put on her shoes and jacket. "Well, I need to run some errands, but I'll pick up some new treats for you while I'm shopping. That sound good?"

But Lulu just stayed in the closet and listened to the sound of the door closing behind Jasmine.

This is fine, she thought. *This is exactly how today was supposed to go, and it's not a big deal that I was going to be posing for glamorous photos all day and instead I am all by myself looking like a failed science project. This is what I wanted all along.*

Lulu took a deep, calming breath and decided to try meditating. She and Jasmine listened to a meditation podcast, so Lulu knew how to do it.

Just try to imagine a beautiful image, she thought. *Come on, Lulu. Any beautiful image will do.*

But she couldn't think of anything, and she couldn't keep the image of her reflection at the salon from popping into her head. After a while of sitting alone and thinking sad thoughts, Lulu heard the sound of Jasmine's footsteps coming back in through the front door. But she was too agitated to run over and lick her friend or sniff any of the treats Jasmine was carrying. She listened to Jasmine's voice coming from the hallway.

♥ *Lulu*

"All right, come on," said Jasmine. "That's enough wallowing. Come out so I can see you."

Lulu didn't want to stop wallowing. She loved to wallow. It was under SPECIAL SKILLS on her résumé. But she didn't want to make Jasmine feel bad. She reluctantly poked her head out of the closet and gasped at what she saw. Jasmine was wearing a brand-new outfit that Lulu had never seen before. It was artsy and abstract, colorful and bizarre. Glittery and blue, but it somehow . . . worked? Jasmine had even stuck up her own hair in weird, pointy directions to look more like Lulu. And she was holding up a smaller, dog-friendly version of the very same outfit. Lulu stood up, and her jaw dropped.

"Now, that's a Big Reaction, girl!" Jasmine said. "So you like it?"

Lulu took it all in. It was weird but undeniably beautiful and, most importantly, totally matched Lulu's new look. Maybe she wasn't the only visionary in the duo, after all.

"You're *art* now, girl," Jasmine said. "And that doesn't change what's on the inside. You're still Lulu. You just have to own your new style! Besides, you've never followed the trends—you *set* them. So come out of there, and let's set them together."

Even though Jasmine was dressed a little like a kooky art teacher, her confidence made her look almost . . . arresting. And Lulu was flattered to see Jasmine go through all the trouble to look so strange, just for her. It was a true BFF move.

Lulu had to admit, the right attitude really brought this look together. If Jasmine was pulling it off, maybe she could make it work too.

"ONE, TWO, THREE . . . so many chairs!" Hugo said. He was sitting on the porch, watching his mom and dad and some neighbors set up tables and chairs in his backyard. "You can count anything, right, Waffles?"

He looked up and saw that he was alone on the porch. Waffles was inside, running around in circles and jumping up and down with Zoe. She had so much energy, while all he wanted to do after their wild afternoon was sit and count chairs.

Waffles had just come back from the groomer, and she looked totally different with her new haircut. Some of her signature floofiness had gotten tangled and matted from all the sugar and goo in the dumpster, so Dad had rushed her in for a last-minute trim.

"Waffles! Whoa. Where'd the rest of Waffles go?" Enrique said as he carried out some more folding chairs into the yard. "You look, like, half the size you used to be!" Hugo laughed because it was true, but then he stopped himself, because he knew Waffles was upset about her new hairstyle. She'd been scratching herself all afternoon. And when Hugo had pointed out that she wouldn't have needed a haircut if she hadn't snuck away and jumped into a dirty dumpster, she'd given him the cold shoulder. She hadn't spoken to him since.

"Hey, Zoe!" Hugo's mom called. "Want to come out here and help me decorate?"

"Ooooh! Can I do the streamers?" Zoe yelled back, excited. "I love streamers!"

"Absolutely!"

Zoe ran outside and started helping the adults put colorful streamers up along the fences. Waffles followed her as far as the porch and sat down to watch, leaving plenty of room between herself and Hugo. Hugo gave her some space, but turned to face her.

"Listen," Hugo started. "I think I owe you an apology. A big one."

Waffles's ears perked up. She was listening.

"I think I've been too hard on you. Too strict," Hugo continued. "I haven't been a good big brother lately, have I?"

"You're a great big brother," Waffles admitted. "But I'm a puppy! And you know what they say: *Puppies gonna puppy!*"

"Do they say that?"

"I do! It's my new saying," Waffles said. "It's just that I have a lot of energy. Like Zoe! I can't sit around all day, napping and counting cars. I need to run around and play and be weird! And that's okay!"

"You're right," Hugo said, the realization washing over him. "You're a kid. You need to act like a kid. As long as nobody's getting hurt, I need to do a better job of letting you act like a kid."

Waffles smiled. Then she rolled over, scooted herself closer to Hugo, and nuzzled him a little with her nose. "Thanks, big bro," she said.

"And by the way," he added, "I know haircuts can be tough. But I think yours looks nice. And plus, it'll grow back!"

Waffles looked super surprised. "It will?!" she yelped. "That's amazing! Why didn't anyone tell me that?"

"I guess that's what big brothers are for."

Hugo thought back to when *he* was a puppy. He used to climb into backpacks and jump up on tables and hide shoes all around the house. Sometimes his silly antics brought the whole family together, giving them stories to tell and laugh about. Hugo looked into the yard and realized that the whole family was laughing right now! Zoe had gotten herself tangled in the streamers. She was having trouble putting them up by herself, but she was clearly having so much fun.

My expectations have been all messed up, Hugo thought as he snuggled Waffles back. *Maybe Waffles can use all that puppy energy for good!*

"Hey, Waff," Hugo said. "Why don't you go help Zoe decorate for the rehearsal dinner?"

"I don't know how to help! And what's a rehearsal dinner? Ooh! Is it like when I eat a treat before dinner to practice for eating dinner?"

"Sort of!" Hugo replied. "You could go down there and help her with the streamers. Grab one end in your mouth and run around the yard!"

"Grab something?! Run?!" Waffles said, jumping up and wagging her tail. "Say no more. I'm in!"

Waffles sprinted down the steps and across the backyard to Zoe. In one quick move, she jumped and grabbed one end of the purple streamers in her mouth.

"Waffles!" Zoe giggled as Waffles ran all over the yard like a maniac with the streamers. Everyone started laughing.

"Look! She's helping decorate!" Dad said, taking out his phone to film a video.

Hugo watched from the porch and smiled as his whole family had fun below.

Puppies gonna puppy, he thought, and wagged his tail.

CHAPTER 10

Lampost?! Mailbox?! Pickle's house?! Big tree?! Park?! School?!

King watched all the familiar landmarks whiz by out the window of the car. But instead of feeling the unbridled joy he usually felt on a car ride, he just felt confused.

Where are we going?!

"In five hundred feet, turn left," the car's voice politely suggested. Jin's mom was driving, and Jin was in the passenger's seat, furiously scribbling something on a pad of paper with a pen.

King tried to think about all the places where they *could* be going. The groomer? No, he'd just had a haircut. The vet? No, he had just been there too! The cheese store to pick out his favorite kind of cheese? Maybe, but that was probably just wishful thinking.

Could he be going to the . . . ? No. He didn't even want to think about the *shelter* word! Whoops. He'd just thought about it. *There's no way, right?* And also, why was there a bag on the seat next to him containing all of his worldly belongings?

Something strange is going on here, he thought.

" 'Erin, I knew as soon as I met you that . . .' What was it?" Jin said as he continued to scratch the pen into the paper.

"You don't remember how you feel?" Jin's mom asked with a smirk as she turned the car onto a ramp and drove them onto the highway. This was the first time King had heard her talk in English.

"No, just the wording!" Jin said. "I had my whole speech for the rehearsal dinner saved on my tablet. Now that it's destroyed, I'm trying to write down as much as I can remember. Oh, and did I tell you the videographer dropped out?"

King could sense that Jin was feeling nervous and stressed, because King knew those feelings really well. In fact, he was feeling them right now! He really wished someone would tell him where they were going.

"I can help with the speech. I remember some," Jin's mom said, calmly trying to help. "You love her! You said that a lot. And a joke about . . . how the house can be smelly, I think?"

"Is that what it was?" Jin fretted. "What was it? It needs to be perfect!"

As King listened to Jin and his mom work on the speech for the rehearsal dinner, he got even more anxious. *Am I supposed to give a speech too?* King wondered. *About Erin? If so, I need time to prepare!*

"Erin feeds me every day!" King barked from the back seat. "Not just in treats and dinner, but also in love!"

Jin and his mom knew two languages very well, but Dog wasn't one of them.

"Not now, King," Jin said. "We're almost there."

Almost where? King pleaded with his eyes. Out the window, King could tell they were downtown now. If they weren't going to the groomer, or the vet, or the cheese store . . . *was* it possible that they were driving to the shelter? King didn't think that Jin seemed angry. He was definitely stressed, but not upset enough to take King to the shelter!

Just then, Jin's mom turned the car left, which King knew was the opposite direction from the shelter, and he breathed a sigh of relief. But he was no less confused. Meanwhile, King caught bits and pieces of the conversation in the front of the car.

"You had that quote. From her favorite movie," Jin's mom said.

"Right. Right . . . but how did it go?" Jin fretted. "This

has to be exactly right. I need her to know how much I love her, you know? That she's so wonderful, and perfect. How much I care about her, and how excited I am every day to even be around her!"

Jin's mom smiled. "So say that."

King was pretty busy worriedly staring out the window, but he couldn't help but feel like the snippets he overheard sounded very nice. It sounded like Jin felt some of the same ways about Erin that King did, which made him happy. But in that moment, he was really just confused. Several minutes and a few more turns later, they parked in a part of the town King didn't recognize. The buildings were unfamiliar, and he didn't smell any trees or fire hydrants that he could use as a landmark.

"Okay," Jin said, tearing the top sheet of paper off the pad. "I think this is in good shape."

Jin carried King out of the car and toward a building, while Jin's mom carried the bag full of King's things. As they got closer to the entrance, King did start to smell something familiar. The unmistakable scent of other dogs. Jin opened a door and took King into some kind of a . . . *place*. A place he'd never been before. A place full of dog smells! Their fur and their pee and their butts and everything.

Maybe this is a store where they sell . . . dog butts?

King thought, but even he knew that probably wasn't a good idea for a store. This place smelled nice. And it looked nice too. Jin put King down on a counter, and King tried to overhear what Jin said to the woman who worked there.

"His name's King."

"Ah, yes. You called earlier. Welcome, King!" The woman started giving King some really good pets, and even a belly rub. "Awww, who's a cute little guy?" she asked.

Well, me—yes. Me. But where am I? King thought.

"Yes! Who's a good boy?"

Me, usually. Most of the time, at least. Today was a little touch and go, but you know how it is. King gave her a desperate look. *But can you please tell me what's going on here?*

"And I think my fiancée dropped off her—our other dog already," King heard Jin say to the nice woman. "Cleo?"

Cleo?! King's mind was racing now. *Cleo's here?!*

"Oh yes!" the woman replied. "She dropped Cleo off just a few minutes before you got here."

She opened up a small gate to a back room, and out walked Cleo. King's tail wagged every which way. He was full of excitement and relief. He still had no idea where he was, but Cleo probably knew!

"Hey, King. Miss me?" Cleo asked.

Jin put King down on the floor while he filled out some paperwork, and King greeted Cleo.

"Oh my gosh! Cleo! I'm so happy to see you!" King exclaimed. "Where are we? What's going on? Have you had dinner? Did you eat chicken? You kind of smell like chicken. Why are we here? Is this a store where they sell dog butts? Or is it a shelter? If so, it's a really fancy shel—"

"Whoa, whoa, slow down, you silly puppy," Cleo said, calm as ever. "I'm happy to see you too. But one question at a time. This isn't a shelter. It's a ken-nel. It's like a hotel for dogs. And it's a really nice hotel too!"

King calmed himself down a little and looked around the room. There were toys everywhere, and everything looked cozy, comfortable, and fun.

"We're just going to be here overnight," Cleo continued. "Erin and Jin are super busy getting ready, and they have the rehearsal dinner tonight. They'll pick us up in the morning, before the wedding!"

King felt so much better. He looked over at Jin, who was still filling out paperwork at the counter. He felt bad for thinking, even for a second, that Jin might take him back to the shelter. Jin was just busy and stressed, and King's behavior today probably didn't help. King understood. After all, he acted a little weird when he was stressed too. In fact, with all of Jin's nervous energy this past week, King wouldn't have been surprised if Jin had run away from home or peed on the floor. But he hadn't, which King thought was really impressive.

Jin's mom noticed Cleo and walked over to introduce herself.

"Oh yeah!" King said. "This is Jin's mom. Jin's mom, this is Cleo!"

Jin's mom gave Cleo some pats for a moment, and then Jin told her it was time for them to leave.

"Come on, we don't want to be late," Jin said as they hurried out the door. He quickly turned back to Cleo and King. "See you guys tomorrow!"

The nice woman leashed up Cleo and King and led them back behind the gate.

"You're going to love our room. We have bunk beds," Cleo said as they walked. "And to answer your other question: Yes, I had chicken for dinner. You know, a champion always eats a hearty dinner at the same time every night."

Oh, how rude of me! King thought. He had been so worked up, he had forgotten to ask Cleo anything about Champion Academy and how her training was going. He was about to think of a good question, but he suddenly noticed something out of the corner of his eye that made him stop in his tracks.

Is that . . . ?

They were walking on the other side of the front desk now, and King spotted a piece of paper sitting on the counter, right near where Jin had been standing. It was his rehearsal dinner speech! He'd left it at the kennel! King figured he must have put it down to fill out those papers and forgotten it.

"King? Why did you stop?" Cleo asked. "Come on, silly. Let's go to our room."

But King didn't move. This was a major problem. What about Jin's speech? What about all those nice things he was going to say about Erin? King wanted their rehearsal dinner to go perfectly!

I know what I have to do, King thought, determined. *I need to get that speech back to Jin.*

So he pulled hard, yanking the leash out of the nice woman's hands, and bolted as fast as he could toward the front desk. He jumped onto a chair, then onto the counter, and grabbed the piece of paper in his mouth.

"King! No!" Cleo barked.

"What?! Oh my—" the nice woman called out.

But he didn't have time to stop, and he didn't have time to explain. King jumped off the counter and sprinted out the door into the crisp night air.

"Jin! Jin! Your speech!" King barked, but he was too late. He turned to see Jin's car pulling away, down the street. Or at least he was pretty sure that was Jin's car. It was getting dark. He didn't have time to make sure. With the speech in his mouth, he started running after it.

"WHO'S A GOOD girl?" Jasmine asked as they walked toward Hugo's house next door.

I am, Lulu thought.

"Who's a perfect doggy?"

That would be me again.

"Who's a stylish work of art and an experimental postmodern comment on beauty standards in the fashion industry through your unconventional haircut and outfit?"

Uhhh, I only know like half of those words, but probably me! Lulu thought. She and Jasmine were both sporting their matching arty look, and they were about to enter Hugo's backyard for the rehearsal dinner. Lulu didn't fully know what that meant, but she knew that rehearsals were for actors, and she obviously loved dinner. She was starting to feel a little bit more confident than she had that afternoon. And she was sitting in her favorite place, Jasmine's arms.

"Okay, Lu. You ready to make a big entrance?"

Lulu licked Jasmine's face.

"I'll take that as a yes," Jasmine said. "Oh, and remember, the YouTube crew is here. Erin told me her videographer dropped out, so I told her I knew a great team to film tonight and tomorrow. And if they get some shots of you too, I'm not complaining!"

Lulu licked her face again.

"Let's do this," Jasmine said, determined.

And so, they strutted into the party and showed off their style. A handful of adults and kids—some neighbors that Lulu recognized, and some strangers—were sitting around tables outside. Everyone turned to look at them.

"Whoa!"

"Quite the look."

"That lady is matching with her dog, and they both look . . . interesting?"

Lulu was usually great at sensing human feelings, but she couldn't tell how the party guests felt about her. Were they . . . *confused*?

"Is that a dog?"

Yeah, that sounds confused, she thought.

All the kids at the party excitedly surrounded her to pet her.

"Wow! She looks so cool!" Enrique, Hugo's human boy, said. "Can I get a selfie with Lulu?"

Okay, at least the kids appreciate what I'm going for, Lulu thought as she posed for a picture with him. *Children really are the best at appreciating both dogs and art. And I live at the intersection of dogs and art. But what about everyone else?*

Lulu recognized the YouTube crew right away. They moved in as Jasmine snapped some selfies with Lulu and pictures of Lulu with the kids. The director pointed at her and whispered something to the camerawoman, who started filming Lulu.

"Wow, that's such a bold look," the woman with the unclear job said. "Both of you. I can't. I just—I really can't."

"Was it . . . intentional?" a neighbor asked, somewhat rudely, as a friend of his looked amused.

"Of course!" Jasmine answered, confident. "Isn't it fabulous?"

As the camerawoman pointed the lens in her direction, Lulu tried to hold her head up high and strut her stuff, but inside, she wasn't quite as self-assured as she was pretending to be.

Hugo and Waffles came up, and Lulu could sense their surprise. *Maybe they're surprised by how great I look!* Lulu tried to tell herself optimistically.

"Lulu! What happened?" Hugo asked, with a genuine look of concern on his face. "Is this the pneumonia?"

"No, no. I'm totally cured. I got a haircut! From a *very* fancy stylist," Lulu responded, still making sure to pose for the camera.

"*That* happened from a *haircut*?" Waffles asked, her eyes wide, as she took in all of Lulu's strange poofy parts, the stars, and the beads. Hugo and Waffles must have realized that they were on the verge of sounding rude, and they quickly started trying to find nice things to say.

"It's not all bad!" Hugo said, trying to sound polite. "I like that little part there, on the side of your neck! And, um . . ." He trailed off.

"It's trendy!" Lulu protested. "At least, I think it might be? Doesn't the outfit help? And did you know that Milan is the new Paris?"

"Who's Paris?" Waffles asked. "Is that the bichon down the street?"

Lulu was getting a bit frustrated. "Well, I'm not the only one here with a bold new haircut," she said, looking at Waffles.

"Oh, thank you!" Waffles replied. "I wasn't sure at first, but I actually feel a lot less hot now. And I can see better without all the floof impeding my vision."

Lulu sighed.

"Don't worry, Lulu," Waffles said. "Did you know that hair grows *back*? Hugo just told me, and it made me feel a lot better."

But Lulu couldn't wait for her hair to get back to normal! Didn't Waffles realize that Lulu was the subject of a *film*? It could make or break her career! Speaking of the film, as Lulu continued to pose for the camera, she could have sworn she heard some crew members laughing about the haircut.

"Can you get a close-up of those weird wisps on her chin?" someone whispered to the camerawoman.

Oh no, Lulu thought. Her biggest fear might be coming true. *What if I can't pull off this look?*

But then, thankfully, Erin entered the backyard, and everyone turned their attention to her and away from Lulu. Erin was the real star of the show tonight, and Lulu was glad to not have the camera in her own face anymore.

"Congratulations!"

"Are you so excited? Tomorrow's going to be perfect."

"How was Champion Academy?"

The humans crowded around Erin, who was smiling from ear to ear. Lulu couldn't help but wag her tail, and momentarily forgot about the stress of how she looked. Erin just seemed so happy, and that made Lulu happy.

A happy person is one of life's greatest pleasures, she thought.

"It was great!" Erin told Hugo's mom. "Cleo learned a lot, and so did I! But now I'm excited to just focus on the wedding."

"I bet you can't wait to see Jin."

"I can't! We've both been so busy. This weekend will be so special. He said he's a few minutes away."

Lulu, Waffles, and Hugo were on the grass underneath a folding table when Jin entered the yard. He was with an older woman who Lulu figured must be his mom. But neither of them looked nearly as happy as Erin. In fact, Jin looked *really* upset, and he was talking on the phone.

"Okay. Okay. Oh my gosh. Okay," Jin said to whoever was inside the phone. "Thank you."

The humans who had been gushing over Erin all looked concerned. Jin hung up the phone. Lulu stood on alert and perked up her ears to hear.

"Jin? Babe?" Erin asked. "What's going on?"

"That was the kennel," Jin said, panic on his face. "King ran away. He's missing."

CHAPTER 11

KING IS MISSING.

Hugo was certain he had misheard Jin at first, but based on Jin's obvious panic, he must have heard right.

"King must have freaked out at the kennel and run off," he said to Lulu and Waffles. "We have to do something! We have to find him. Let's sneak out!"

"No way," said Waffles. She was still shaken from her dumpster misadventure.

"Waffles, there's one rule I haven't told you about," said Hugo, dramatically staring off into the darkening sky.

"What's that?"

"The rule is . . ." He paused. "If another dog is in trouble . . . there are no rules." Hugo had to admit he felt pretty cool saying there weren't any rules. He wished he could have said it with a stick hanging out of his mouth or a pair of sunglasses on. That would have been even cooler.

136 🦴 Hugo

"Well, I think it's a great idea," said Lulu. "As you know, I *live* for drama. I don't think Jin or Jasmine or your family will notice if we leave—they're all too busy stressing about King."

Hugo looked around. It was true. Jasmine was on the porch, pacing. His mom and dad were huddled with some other humans, trying to come up with a human plan. They had no idea the dogs were making a plan of their own.

"The only *real* problem is," Lulu continued, "I sort of have a camera crew following me right now, and they're sort of, like, obsessed with me. *They* might notice."

"I think I know what would get them to stop paying attention to you," offered Waffles solemnly.

"What could possibly distract them from *moi*?" asked Lulu.

"Well, there's only one thing people like more than dogs," said Waffles. "And that's . . . puppies."

Lulu gasped. "Well played, Waffles," she said. "You're right. Compared with you, I'm yesterday's news. Puppies are like catnip for humans. But we need to help you play the part. Where do your people keep the wardrobe around here?"

Hugo led them to a bin in the corner of the yard that was full of toys. He felt a bit uncomfortable digging through this stuff. Knowing the difference between a kid toy and a dog toy was something he prided himself on, but he knew this was for a good cause. Lulu pulled out one of Zoe's dolls, and Hugo cocked his head to the side.

"How's that going to help?" he asked.

Lulu took the doll's hat off and placed it on Waffles's head. "There," she proclaimed. "Now we're in business. Puppies in hats are absolute gold. They just featured one on the cover of *Dogue* magazine."

"*Dogue*?" Waffles asked, adjusting the hat.

"It's *Vogue* for dogs," snapped Lulu. "Stay with me. Now listen closely. You're a cute puppy, Waffles. But there's a difference between a *cute puppy* and a *smol pupper*, and those guys out there aren't going to settle for anything less than the sweetest, *smollest* pupper they've ever seen. They're professionals, after all. This is important. Be present, and honest, and prepared. Bark from your diaphragm. And remember, *Big Reactions.*"

Hugo groaned. He was pretty sure Waffles could have handled the distraction without a full acting lesson, but Lulu really did live for drama, and right now she was in her element.

"Head back," Lulu directed. "Feet floppy. Tail waggy. Spin in circles?"

Waffles started spinning.

"Faster? Faster! Slower. Faster. Yes, good! You're ready."

As soon as they stepped away from the toy bin,

the cameras swarmed around Lulu. Then, as planned, Waffles took a few steps away and started yelping. A few of the crew members turned toward her just as Waffles started spinning in circles. Hugo had to admit it was *adorable*. He looked over at Lulu and could have sworn she had a tear in her eye.

"She's magnificent," Lulu whispered.

Before they knew it, the whole YouTube crew was surrounding Waffles while she ran around deliriously in circles, jumped up and down, and made her cutest possible puppy faces. Hugo watched proudly as Waffles rolled over several times in a row, doing it perfectly, the way he showed her.

"I taught her that part," he murmured to Lulu as they slowly inched away.

"Who *is* that dog?" Hugo heard one of the crew members exclaim.

"That dog's got a face for the camera," another one shouted. "And I think I saw a hat like that in *Dogue!*"

The attention successfully on Waffles, Hugo and Lulu made a run for the gate. Thankfully, someone at the party had left it wide open in all the confusion, and they were able to walk right through. Then they ran a few blocks away to make sure they weren't spotted before stopping to make a plan.

"Okay, let's think!" Lulu said. "If we were King, where would we go?"

"Well," Hugo started, thinking hard, "Jin said he was last seen at the kennel. Shouldn't we go there?"

"I don't know where that kennel is, do you?" Lulu made a very good point. "Plus, King could be miles from there by now. Come on, if you were King, where would you go?"

Hugo thought about it. His own happy place was at home with his family, and if he ever escaped from a kennel, he'd probably try to find his way back to the house. Lulu was apparently thinking the same thing.

"Erin's house," they barked in unison. So they walked through several backyards, avoiding detection, until they got to Erin's backyard. Hugo circled the house and saw that all the lights were off, the laundry room window was closed, and there was no sign of King or anyone.

"The park!" Lulu said. "That's the other place he loves the most. And it's between here and downtown."

"You're right," Hugo replied. "King loves the park more than I love my Fuzzy Bunny. *Maybe* he's there."

As they silently made their way to the park, the reality of what they were doing started to set in.

King was missing, and pretty soon the humans might realize Hugo and Lulu were missing too. Hugo hated to make his family worry, but sometimes a dog had to take matters into his own paws. He couldn't believe this was the second rescue mission he'd been on in one day. He tried to shake off his worries and focus on King instead. But when they got to the park, their friend was still nowhere to be found. They searched the lawn, the fountain, and the dog run, but there was no scent of him anywhere.

"Oh, hey, dogs," a small voice piped up from a tree branch above them. It was Nuts. "You haven't seen my acorns, have you?"

"No, Nuts, we haven't," Lulu replied.

Nuts sighed. "Figures," he said. "Boy, oh boy. I'll tell ya, things with Berries aren't going any better than they were the last time I saw you. It's like we have nothing in common. I mean, sure, we both like trees. But who doesn't? I'm trying to get her into Frisbees, but she has no interest whatsoever. And you know me, Frisbees are sort of my whole thing. I can't get enough of them! But you know, they're not for playing. They're for *collecting*. If you play with them, you devalue—"

"Enough!" Lulu yelped. "We're not here to chat. We're having an emergency! King is missing!"

To Hugo's surprise, a look of genuine concern crossed Nuts's face. They filled him in on the story, and when they were done, he nodded thoughtfully.

"This sounds serious," he finally said, with a shocking amount of gravity. "I haven't seen your friend. But if you want, I can activate the Squirrel Network."

"The what now?" Lulu was confused, but Hugo figured any kind of help was good.

"Yes," he said. "Do that. Whatever that means."

Nuts jumped into action. He hopped to the ground, pulled out an acorn, and started tapping an elaborate code onto the base of his tree. He looked like some sort of bushy-tailed secret agent. Immediately, another squirrel popped out from a nearby tree: It was Berries!

"Berries," Nuts shouted up to her. "Good, you got my message."

"Nuts," she shouted down. "Did you mean to send out a code orange?"

"Affirmative," he responded, all business. "Missing dog. Repeat. Missing dog. Name's King. He's a mix, part border collie. About yea high."

Nuts jumped about a foot and a half off the ground as he said that last part. Then he continued. "This dog is young, silly, and weird. Last seen at a kennel downtown. Pass it along."

Berries nodded, took out an acorn of her own, and started tapping the same message on her tree. "Squirrel Network. Activate. Missing dog. Repeat. Missing dog."

She repeated the details about King, and the dogs soon heard the message echoing throughout the entire park.

"Missing dog. Missing dog. Pass it along. Pass it along. A mix, part border collie. Missing dog."

It was actually sort of beautiful, Hugo thought, watching the message being carried through the park and, they assumed, through the town. Who knew the squirrels were this sophisticated? And interconnected? He looked at Lulu, stunned, and they waited eagerly for the Squirrel Network to bring back a clue.

Where are you, King? Hugo wondered.

KING HAD ABSOLUTELY no idea where he was. He had chased Jin's car as far as he could, running as fast as possible, but he hadn't been able to keep up. Now it was dark, and he was in a part of town he'd never seen before. He didn't recognize any hydrants or lampposts or mailboxes. He sniffed some of the doors of storefronts and apartment buildings, seeing if he could find a familiar smell, but no luck.

Well, I'm officially lost, King thought.

"Eshcuth me!" he barked at a nearby pigeon. He still had Jin's speech in his mouth, so his barks were a bit muffled. "D'you know how th'get to Hugo'th housh?"

But the pigeon ignored him and flew away.

"Hugo'th housh? Anyone?" he yelped at a bush, just in case someone was inside it. "Duth anyone know Hugo?"

But either nobody was inside the bush, or nobody inside the bush knew Hugo, because he didn't get a response. King knew that if he could just somehow get to the rehearsal dinner and give Jin the speech, everything would be okay. That was, if his nervous slobbers weren't ruining it.

Think, King, think! King thought. *Good, King! You're thinking about thinking. That's a start!*

He tried to come up with some kind of clue that might help him get to Hugo's house.

Think really hard, King! You can do this. Don't get distracted by any smells, like you usually— Wait! That's it! Smells! I'm a genius!

King had a plan! If he could think about one specific smell at the rehearsal dinner, maybe he could search for that smell until he got to Hugo's house. But what smell could that be?

What was Jin stressing out about the other day, on the phone? He said the food at the rehearsal dinner was going to be . . .

King paced in circles as he tried to remember. *Was it turkey? Cereal? Bread?* King thought about all the different types of human food he knew.

Salmon! It was salmon! King remembered. Yes! That was the word Jin kept saying into the phone.

And King was pretty sure that salmon was a fish, because he'd watched a nature documentary with Erin once. King definitely knew what fish smelled like, and he hated it. Erin had tried to feed him a fish-based dinner once, and he'd refused to eat it because of the horrid scent. Cleo loved it, but King barked a strong "no, thank you." He knew he would remember that stink forever. Now, as he wandered through the unfamiliar streets, he almost threw up just thinking about it.

But he would do anything to get back to Erin, give Jin his speech, and save their big party. Even if it meant seeking out a terrible smell. So he sniffed and sniffed, wandering from one strange block to another, until finally—he smelled fish!

There you are! he thought. *But where are you coming from?*

He followed the smell, sticking his nose up and down and all around as he scurried through the streets. He figured he must be getting close to Hugo's house. How many fish smells could there be in the world?

The fish smell got stronger and stronger, and soon King found himself in a parking lot next to a building he'd never seen before. In the darkness he couldn't even tell what kind of a building it was. He followed the scent all the way to the back of the building, up a couple of steps, and to a broken screen door.

Hmm . . . this smells like salmon, but it isn't Hugo's house, King thought, confused. *Where am I?*

"Intruders are not welcome," a silky voice called out from the other side of the door. "What's the password?"

Password?! King panicked. He didn't know any passwords, and he wasn't even sure if he wanted to go inside. But he thought maybe whoever was on the other side of the door could help him find Hugo's house, so he let go of the speech from his mouth and blurted out the first thing that came into his head.

"Salmon?" King barked.

There was a moment of silence, and then a creaking sound. A paw slowly pushed the door open, and two big eyes peered out from the darkness.

"Well, well, well . . . what do we have here?" the voice asked.

"Um, I'm King," he replied nervously. "I'm looking for my friend's house."

"And you brought salmon, you say?"

King wasn't sure how to respond. He didn't have

salmon, and he didn't want to lie. But he also didn't want this creature to leave him alone without any help. "I, uh, well, you see," King tried to deflect. But then he nodded.

Did I just nod? Whoops, King thought. Sometimes his head did all sorts of weird things when he was nervous.

"I'll take that as a yes," the smooth voice replied. "Come on in."

And just like that, a pair of paws lunged out, grabbed him by the face, and yanked him through the broken screen.

Ow! That kinda hurt! King remembered that Jin's speech was sitting outside on the step. Wherever he was now, he knew he'd have to make it quick and grab the speech on the way out.

The inside of this building was dark—even darker than the night outside. And the smell of fish was stronger too. It was just as gross as he remembered, and now it was overwhelming. Several pairs of bright, glowing eyes stared back at him.

"Where am I?" King whined softly into the abyss.

Suddenly, the lights came on. He was in a bright white square room lined with cages. King thought it kind of looked like the back room of the vet. Except there were no people. And no dogs. And all the cages were open. And most notably, the entire room was filled with cats!

So that's who the eyes and voice belonged to . . .

There were cats everywhere. They were on the floor, and on tables, and on chairs. They were high up on shelves, glaring down at him. One was on a counter by the wall and had clearly just flicked the light switch on. The cats on the floor were circling King now, and getting closer. One rubbed its body into King's side, making strange eye contact with him the whole time. Another cat pounced in out of nowhere, booped him on the nose, and then returned to the corner of the room.

King tried to stay calm, but he had never seen this many cats in one place before—except for in a strange and terrifying movie Erin watched once, where they were all dancing. But this was real life, and it was very intimidating. There were bowls of half-finished cat food all over the floor. If the smell wasn't bad enough, the sight of all that gloopy, mushy fish was even worse.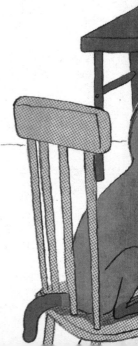

So that explains the fish smell, King thought, looking away from the bowls. *But what is this place?*

He could also smell the distinct smell of humans. But he didn't see any. "Where are all the people?" he asked.

A ginger tabby slowly stepped forward, right into King's face. She spoke with the same voice that King had heard at the door. "The people go home at six, honey. Five on Fridays. The cats are in charge now."

King slowly backed away from her. He was terrified. "Th-this was a m-mistake," King stammered. "I'm sorry. I should go!"

As he turned around and stepped toward the door, the tabby stepped in front of him, and two other cats joined her, blocking his path.

"Oh, doggy," the tabby purred. "We're not ready to let you go just yet. Don't you know where you are?"

She gestured behind her to a sign on the wall. He looked at it, then back at the tabby, and shrugged. Unfortunately, the sign was just letters and words, no helpful pictures that might help King understand what he was looking at.

"I don't think he can read," another cat whispered to the tabby.

"Oh, right," she said, turning back to King. "It says, 'Hotel Catifornia—Luxe Accommodations for Your Kitty.'"

"We're the kitties," another cat meowed. "And you're standing in *our* luxe accommodations."

"Hotel *Catifornia*?" King repeated hesitantly.

"That's right. You can check out anytime you like," the tabby explained. "But you can never leave."

The other cats surrounded King and inched even closer. "Now, let's talk about that salmon you brought."

Uh-oh.

CHAPTER 12

LULU AND HUGO ran through the narrow city streets.

"King? King?" Lulu barked into every alleyway and around every corner as they followed the Squirrel Network's intelligence. They'd been passed off from one squirrel to the next, each having spotted King on a different part of his journey.

A squirrel popped out from a bush in front of them. "This block right here," the squirrel announced. "This is where your friend was last seen."

"Are you sure?" Hugo asked.

The squirrel gave him a stern look. "The Squirrel Network is always sure." Then the squirrel darted away, disappearing back into the bush.

Lulu and Hugo walked up and down the block, looking everywhere for King.

"King? Buddy?" Hugo barked. "Where are you?"

Lulu yelped his name as loud as she could at every door they passed, but he didn't come out.

"Do you think the squirrels were wrong?" Hugo asked.

"Nuts said that the squirrels see *everything*," Lulu replied. "EVERYTHING." Actually, now that Lulu really thought about that, it was kind of creepy. "Anyway, the point is, if King had left this block, the squirrels would have told us."

Hugo nodded, and they kept sniffing around for any hint of King they could find.

"Something in this parking lot smells familiar," Hugo said. Lulu joined him in sniffing the ground in the mostly empty concrete rectangle. "Is that a whiff of King I'm detecting?"

Then Lulu spotted something, and her eyes went wide with horror. "Oh no," she said. Across the parking lot, there was a sign on the side of a building. Lulu could make it out clearly:

HOTEL CATIFORNIA- LUXE ACCOMMODATIONS FOR YOUR KITTY

"Uh-oh." Hugo followed her gaze and saw the sign now too. Lulu knew that Hugo could also read.

"They make special kennels just for cats?"

"I guess so," Hugo said, nodding. "Let's be careful."

They kept following King's smell until Lulu spotted something else: a piece of paper that smelled more like King than anything else in the parking lot. It was sitting on the steps up to a broken screen door leading into the cat hotel.

"Hugo, look," Lulu said. She nudged the paper toward Hugo and he sniffed it.

His eyes lit up. "No question. That's been in King's mouth," he said.

"You don't think he's . . . ," Lulu started. Then she noticed Hugo was staring at a hole in the screen door.

"That hole in the screen is *kind of* shaped like King," Hugo said. "That, and the piece of paper, and if the squirrels are as accurate as they say . . . I think he's in there."

"But what would King want with a bunch of cats?" Lulu said. She had a thought and got even more scared. "Or what could a bunch of cats want with King?"

"Only one way to find out." Hugo turned toward the door and howled, "King! Are you in there?"

There was a muffled whine from somewhere inside the building. But it was drowned out by several loud yowls. Lulu shuddered and shared a concerned look with Hugo.

"That settles it," Lulu said. "King's in there. He's been dognapped! But why?"

"If I know anything about cats," Hugo replied, "it's that they do a lot of things that have no reason or explanation. We could waste our lives asking why. All I know is we need to go in there and save him."

Hugo bravely started up the steps toward the door, but Lulu stopped him.

"Wait!" she called. "We can't go in there. They're *cats,* Hugo. We have no idea how many. Pickle's bad enough, and she's just one cat. They'll tear us apart. Physically, mentally, and other ways I don't even know about yet. Plus, they might make fun of my haircut." After the way the humans had reacted at the rehearsal dinner, cats were the *last* things Lulu wanted weighing in on her new style.

"Well, we have to do *something*!" Hugo said.

Lulu looked around the parking lot and the rest of the storefronts on the block. Something felt familiar about this neighborhood. *Hmm,* she thought. *Hmm* was what she liked to think when she was thinking. *Aha! I know what to do!* "Follow me," Lulu said confidently. "I have an idea."

She led the way out of the parking lot and down the block as Hugo followed close behind.

"I just hope we're not too late," Lulu said as she turned the corner, sniffing the ground for familiar landmarks. *I know it's around here somewhere,* she thought as they walked a couple more blocks. That's when they passed the glass covering of the bus stop. She'd been here just yesterday.

"We're close," Lulu said, her tail wagging. "I know the way from here!"

"The way to where?!" Hugo said, panting as they ran. She hadn't explained her idea to him, because she wasn't even sure if it would work. But she had to try! Finally, she spotted it. GROÖM, her usual salon.

Hugo looked confused. "Listen, Lulu. I know you're self-conscious about your hair, but now's not the time to—"

"Don't be silly!" Lulu said, and she pushed the front door open. "Come on."

Hugo trailed into the salon behind her. The place was empty except for Beverly, the substitute groomer, who was too busy packing up her things to notice the dogs.

Pickle slowly sauntered out of the back room.

"There she is," Lulu said.

SO THIS WAS Lulu's plan, Hugo thought. *Get Pickle's help! Pretty smart, actually.*

"I'll be right back, Pickle! Just grabbing a bite to eat," the woman with the glasses said. Then she walked out of the salon, leaving Hugo, Lulu, and Pickle alone.

"Wait, what's Pickle doing at a salon for dogs?" Hugo asked.

"It's a long story," Lulu replied.

"Not really," Pickle replied, turning to them. "My owner is the substitute groomer this week. Now, what are *you two* doing here? Looking for a bath and a trim?"

"No," Lulu said defiantly. "We need your help!"

"King is trapped at that cat kennel, Hotel Catifornia!" Hugo explained.

Pickle shuddered. "Those cats are serious," she said.

"Can you help us rescue King?" Lulu pleaded. "We need to get back to Erin and Jin's rehearsal dinner. You're a cat—maybe they'll listen to you."

"What's in it for me?" Pickle asked, casually licking her leg.

Hugo looked at Lulu. She seemed unsure. But he had an idea. "Well," Hugo said, "the rehearsal dinner is at my house, and I'm sure there's going to be some leftover salmon. I might be able to bring you some."

Pickle's eyes lit up.

"And we need help from *you*," Lulu continued, "because you're obviously the smartest and best cat! We know you're the only one who can help us."

Pickle's eyes lit up even more. "Okay, I'll help," she announced, and she walked toward the front of the salon, where Hugo and Lulu were standing. "But we need to go now, before Beverly gets back."

As Pickle approached them, Hugo could tell she was getting a better look at Lulu's haircut and outfit. After taking it all in for a minute, the cat gave an approving nod.

"Your look is actually kind of impressive," Pickle said. "At least it's a *statement*."

Lulu's tail rose, but she stayed focused on the task at hand. She turned and determinedly led the way out of GROÖM. Hugo followed behind her, and Pickle behind him.

When they got back to Hotel Catifornia, Lulu cautiously approached the broken screen door.

"Intruders are not welcome!" a voice called from the other side of the door. "What's the password?"

Lulu glanced at Hugo for help, but he just shrugged. The only password he knew was *HugoDog492!*, which was Mom's password for her typing rectangle. That probably wouldn't help here.

But Pickle sidled up to the door and gave the dogs a look that said, *I've got this.* She cleared her throat. "The password is . . . *I'm a cat!*" Pickle hissed, and pounced right through the hole in the screen door.

Lulu nervously looked at Hugo, then followed Pickle through the door.

"Oh, I don't know if I'll fit through that—" Hugo started, but Lulu was one step ahead of him. She turned and gave the door a good push so that it swung open. Hugo stepped through, joining Lulu and Pickle in the kitty kennel.

It took Hugo's eyes a minute to adjust, but once they did, he took in the room. There were cats all over the place, on every possible surface. Across the room, the wall was lined with cages. They were all open, except for one.

"King!" Lulu shouted. "There you are! Are you okay?"

Sure enough, King was inside the cage, and the door was closed. The cats must have figured out how to unlock their own pens, and then trapped King in one of them. He looked sad and scared. He was sitting on his tail with his head on his paws, but he perked up when he heard Lulu's high-pitched yelp.

"Lulu! Hugo! You came to—AH-CHOO!" One of the cats guarding his cage had flicked King's nose with her tail through the cage door.

Pickle meowed loudly and got the attention of all the other cats. "Excuse me! Where are the humans who run this establishment?"

A confident ginger tabby stepped forward. Hugo could tell by how the other cats avoided direct eye contact that she was their leader, the dominant one.

"The humans went home for the night," the tabby said as she circled Pickle, Lulu, and Hugo. "You three should get going too, if you know what's good for you."

"We're here for the dog," Pickle explained. "Will you let him go?"

"Oh, *that* dog?" the tabby said nonchalantly, tossing a look back at King. "He came in here and promised us salmon."

"Wow, that's a very bold promise to make," Pickle said, looking directly at Hugo. "A dog wouldn't want to promise a cat salmon if he couldn't deliver."

"We're going to keep him here overnight to teach him a lesson," the tabby explained, and as she got closer to Hugo, he could see that her collar said QUEEN PRINCESS.

"That's a very clever idea," Pickle said. "Listen, my name's Pickle, and I happen to know that dog. I'm not surprised that he got on your nerves. He's annoying and

Hugo

silly and stinky, and sometimes I wish *I* could lock him up in a—"

"Psst!" Lulu nudged Pickle and gave her a look, urging her to get back on topic.

"But these are his friends, and they'd really like to get him back," Pickle pleaded. "Please."

Queen Princess stopped circling them and stood still for a moment, as if she was thinking. Then she looked Pickle right in the eyes. "No," she declared.

"Huh," Pickle huffed. "You cats are acting like a bunch of . . . of . . . *hairbrushes*. Why so grumpy? Did someone give you a belly rub this morning, tabby?"

"The only thing rubbing me the wrong way is you, kitty," Queen Princess growled back. "Who do you think you are? Coming into *our* territory, with a couple of dogs"—Queen Princess smirked at Lulu's hairstyle—"if that's even what that one is."

Lulu snarled and tried to look intimidating, but Hugo stepped in front of her.

"Please, Miss, uh, Princess," Hugo started.

"It's *Queen* Princess!" Queen Princess growled, turning her attention back to Pickle. "You *fireworks* better get out of here."

"Don't be such a *car ride*," Pickle snapped back. "You smell like *mustard*."

Hugo and Lulu exchanged confused looks. *Car ride? Mustard?* Every time he was around Pickle, Hugo felt like he learned new cat swear words. As the cats kept arguing, he didn't understand half of their insults, but he could tell the tension in the room was building. The other cats were closing in on them, getting closer and closer. So he tried to defuse the situation.

"Hey, everybody!" he piped up. "My name's Hugo. What if we all just calmed down, acted like good dogs and cats, and settled this rationally, with a nice old-fashioned wrestle?"

Everyone just stared back at him blankly.

"So, is that a yes? Should we wrestle—?"

"Have a seat, dog," Pickle said, shooting him a withering glare. "I'll handle this."

Hugo nodded and sat down. He wasn't one to ignore a request to sit.

"Good boy," Pickle said, and then she turned to the other cats. "Let's talk."

Hugo and Lulu watched as Pickle huddled up with Queen Princess and a few of the other Hotel Catifornia guests. They were speaking in whispers, so Hugo couldn't hear, and it seemed like they were negotiating.

"What do you think they're saying?" Lulu asked.

"I don't know," Hugo said, concerned. He glanced over at King and tried to give his friend a hopeful look, but he wasn't sure he felt hopeful.

When Pickle came out of the huddle, she also looked uncertain.

"What happened?" Lulu asked. "What did they say?"

Pickle took a deep breath. "They want to settle this with a Cat Battle," she said.

"A Cat Battle?" Hugo asked. "What's that?"

"It's like a rap battle, but with a little bit more whimsy and dancing. And the occasional scratch."

Hugo's mouth fell open. Cats, dancing? It reminded him of a strange movie he had watched with Sofia a few months back, and he shuddered.

"One-on-one. Tournament-style. Three rounds," Pickle explained. "Now, sit back and watch how it's done."

The boarded cats discussed among themselves and chose three representatives, including Queen Princess, to go up against Pickle in the Cat Battle. The first cat stepped forward. He was a British shorthair with a gray coat and big round eyes. The other cats encircled him and Pickle, watching intently.

"Whiskers, ears, paws, and tail," the gray cat rapped. "I've got them all and I never fail! You can't rhyme, you can only purr. It's because you're so distracted by my gorgeous fur."

He finished his freestyle by whacking Pickle with his tail, and the cats in the circle jumped and danced in celebration. But Pickle barely reacted. She looked as confident as ever.

"My name is Pickle, feel my wrath," she replied. "I'm scarier than a stranger or a bath! I've got strong hind legs, and I'm ready to start kickin'. You remind me of my breakfast because you're such a chicken."

"Whoa! Nice!" The other cats couldn't believe it.

Hugo was impressed. Pickle's rudeness made her oddly talented at Cat Battles, it seemed. And who knew she was such a good rhymer? Lulu's eyes were glued to the competition too. She seemed fascinated.

"Pickle wins round one," Queen Princess announced. "May the next cat step forward."

The next cat was a tiny Persian kitten with big poofy hair. She rhymed with a high-pitched, squeaky voice. "You might think I'm just a kitty, but I'm actually pretty gritty, and when I look at you, all I feel is . . . pity! I wish I had a *nickel* for every time I destroyed a *Pickle*!"

The kitty finished and paced to the side arrogantly. But Hugo just shrugged. That one didn't make as much sense. Was the idea that she often destroys pickles? Also, what would a cat want with a nickel?

Pickle stepped forward, stretched out her legs, and looked the kitty in the eyes. "Everybody here knows I'm gonna *beat you*," Pickle meowed. "You're as tiny as a mouse, so I bet that I could *eat you*! You might be furry and you might be *cute*, but hang out with you? I'd rather *smell a fruit*."

"*Ohhhhh!* Harsh!" The cats around the circle reacted as if their minds had been blown yet again. Pickle won round two.

Hugo turned to Lulu, confused. "I guess cats don't like the smell of fruit?"

She looked puzzled too. Then they turned back to the center of the circle because it was time for the final showdown. Queen Princess stepped forward.

She cleared her throat, and all the cats listened intently. "You've had a good run, but this is where it *ends*. You should have stayed at home with your *canine friends*.

What color is your fur—is it brown or is it mink? You remind me of my litter box—you *litter*-ally stink."

Queen Princess held her nose in the air. The other cats yowled in celebration.

Hugo was worried now. That was a tough one to beat. But Pickle stepped forward and commanded everyone's attention.

"When Pickle starts to rhyme, get ready for rejection. I've got nine lives and each one is *purr*-fection. You might be *hairier*, but I'm *scarier* than a *cat carrier*. Don't mess with me or I'll unleash my . . . my . . ."

Uh-oh. It looked like Pickle couldn't think of a rhyme. But out of nowhere, Lulu jumped forward.

"Terrier!" Lulu barked, finishing the line with flair. Then she got up in Queen Princess's face and kept it going. "Queen? Princess? Which one is it? This hotel gets no stars, because I hated my visit. Oh, and—you just admitted that your litter box stinks! That means it's full of *poop*! Doesn't your human know how to *scoop*?"

Wow, that was incredible! Hugo thought. He looked at King, who was excitedly wagging his tail and cheering loudly.

Queen Princess seemed stunned. Hugo assumed she had never lost a Cat Battle, and especially not to a dog.

She huddled with a few other cats, then looked over at Pickle. "You've won," Queen Princess said solemnly. "Congratulations."

Pickle turned to Lulu. "Thanks for the assist," she purred. "Nice rhymes."

And just like that, the cats opened King's cage, and he ran over to Lulu and Hugo. King excitedly licked their faces and sniffed their butts. Hugo playfully wrestled him back, excited that his friend was safe and sound.

"You saved me! Thank you! Thank you!" King barked, and then he tentatively turned to Pickle. "And thank you too!"

"I'm surprised they kept their word and actually let him go," Lulu said.

"Of course they did," Pickle said, nodding respectfully to the other cats, who nodded back. "The rules of a Cat Battle are sacred."

Hugo, Lulu, King, and Pickle left through the hole in the screen door and walked into the parking lot under the dark night sky.

"What were you doing here in the first place, King?" Lulu asked, echoing the exact question Hugo had been thinking.

"Jin left his speech at the kennel, and I needed to get it back to him," King explained. "Then I got lost and— Wait, where's the speech?!"

"You mean that wet, crumpled-up piece of paper we found out here?" Lulu asked. "Don't worry. I hid it in that bush so it would be safe."

King looked relieved. He happily retrieved the piece of paper from the bush. "Now lesh guh back t' the rehearthal dunn," he said, barely able to talk through the paper.

"Yep, let's get back to my house!" Hugo said, leading the way. "But first . . ." He turned to Pickle, who was walking the other way, toward her owner at the salon. "Thanks again for the help, Pickle. You were really impressive in there. We owe you some leftover salmon."

Pickle nodded regally. "I'll add it to the list of things you owe me," she said, walking away with her head held high. "Plus, it's always good to brush up on my Cat Battle skills."

"Lesh go!" King barked. "Before Jin needth hith thpeech!"

So Hugo, Lulu, and King ran as fast as they could back home.

CHAPTER 13

WHEN THEY GOT to Hugo's house, the gate was open. King followed Hugo and Lulu into the backyard. There were tables and chairs and all kinds of decorations. There were a few humans, but a lot of empty seats. He didn't see any sign of Erin or Jin.

"There aren't as many people here as when we left," Hugo said.

Oh no, King thought. *Are we too late?*

Then he noticed a handful of humans he didn't recognize. Two of them were holding cameras and pointing them right at Waffles, who was off in the corner of the yard, rolling around and wiggling her legs every which way. The humans with the cameras were laughing and loving it. Hugo's human sister Zoe was getting in on the action too.

"We're doing cartwheels," Zoe shouted to the cameras as she tumbled on the ground with Waffles.

King set the speech down on the grass so he could talk. "What's up with that?" he asked Hugo and Lulu.

"That's just Waffles being Waffles," Lulu explained. "We asked her to do her best puppy routine as a distraction so we could get out to find you and nobody would notice we were gone."

"Ah, the old King trick," King said, remembering the time he did the same thing to help get Napoleon, Waffles, and Pickle out of the shelter. "Good idea." Then he saw that the handful of other people who were in the yard all looked upset. He thought he heard one of them say his name.

"I hope they find him soon," King overheard, and he realized they *weren't* too late after all. The dinner must have been put on hold because of him. Erin and Jin probably went to look for him, along with a lot of the other guests. King suddenly felt a pang of regret, knowing that he had derailed the party, but he couldn't help but feel a bit touched as well. Erin and Jin really did care about him, enough to pause their own dinner until they found him. King understood what a big deal that was, because there were very few things that would make him take a break from eating dinner.

King gave a big, loud bark to get everyone's attention.

The remaining guests turned their heads, and Hugo's dad came running right away with outstretched arms. "There you are! They're back! And King! It's King!"

Hugo's dad knelt down, gave all three dogs the biggest hug, and gave King some especially good rubs. All the people in the yard breathed a huge collective sigh of relief.

"Oh, King, thank goodness!" Hugo's dad said. "We were all so worried about you."

The other people in the yard rushed over. Hugo's mom was talking on her cell phone on the porch, and turned to see the amazing doggy lovefest. "They're back! King's here! He found his way back!" she said into the phone. "Tell everyone to come back to the house!"

Then she joined in on the big group hug. "Awww, buddy," Hugo's mom said, petting King's chin. "You must have missed Erin so much that you ran all the way back to the neighborhood!"

It felt good to be showered with this much love and attention, King thought as more guests returned to the backyard. One by one, Erin's friends and neighbors gave him incredible pets. Nobody seemed mad at all, just relieved that King was safe.

"There you are!"

King turned to see Cleo's tall, strong legs leaping toward him, and she was pulling an ecstatic Erin with her. Upon seeing Erin, King felt a flood of happy feelings and wanted to jump all over her forever. So he did! Or at least until she sat up and started giving him some of the best pets he'd ever felt. The pets from the party guests were great, King thought, but there was no pet like a pet from *Erin*.

"Oh, King! You scared us, you silly little guy," Erin said. "I'm so, so happy to see you. Did you run all the way back here from town?"

Twice in one day, King thought as he nuzzled into Erin's lap. Then he cocked his head toward Cleo. "How did *you* get here?" King asked her.

"Erin came and checked me out of the kennel as soon as she heard you were gone," Cleo explained. "Then we walked all around trying to find you! I was sniffing everywhere." Cleo stuck her nose toward him. "You smell like cats," she said.

King, Lulu, and Hugo shared a look.

"We'll tell you all about it later," King said. "And see! I have Jin's speech!"

King picked up the speech in his mouth and showed her.

Cleo seemed genuinely surprised and impressed. "Wow," she said. "You're one weird dog, King. But I have to give you credit for getting all the way back here with the speech intact. Oh, speaking of Jin!"

King stood up from Erin's lap to see Jin walking toward them. King was worried—would Jin be mad that he ran off again, after everything that happened today? He wished he could tell Jin he was sorry for making everyone leave the rehearsal dinner because of him.

But he didn't need to worry, because Jin immediately dropped to his knees and rubbed King all over his body. Jin gave King the kind of belly rub that made King wish he could give Jin a belly rub right back to return the favor, but he had tried that on people before and his paws were never big enough, unless the person was a baby.

"Oh man, am I happy to see you!" Jin said.

King dropped the speech at Jin's feet.

"What's . . . ? You didn't . . . did you?" Jin said, picking up the paper and uncrumpling it. "You couldn't have. *No way!* Wow, King. I don't even know what to say except that you're a very, very good boy."

King may have been in Hugo's backyard, but sitting there with Cleo and getting incredible pets from both Jin and Erin, he really felt at home.

KING SPENT THE rest of the rehearsal dinner sitting underneath the kids' table because it was the best spot to score some cheese. Enrique and Sofia were being very generous and dropping slices every few minutes. King felt like the night had been a success. Everyone was talking and eating and having fun. Erin and Jin both finally looked relaxed after their long week.

Clink clink clink! Jin tapped on the side of his glass with a fork.

King perked up. "I know what that sound means," he said. "He wants me to run around and bark."

"No, silly," Cleo said. "It's time for his speech."

King and Cleo moved closer to hear as Jin took out the half-chewed, slobber-covered piece of paper and started to read aloud.

"'Erin, I knew as soon as I met you that . . .'" He paused.

Whoops, King thought. *Maybe I chewed it so much that he can't read it!*

Jin folded up the paper and put it away. He looked at Erin. "I was so nervous that I wrote out a whole speech." Jin laughed. "But I'd rather speak from the heart, you know? Erin, you're the best person I know. I just love you so much, and I'm so excited to be a family together. Me, you, Cleo, and King."

Jin smiled at King and Cleo. "Those two unbelievable dogs," he continued. "I don't know how, but I somehow left them out of the original speech. Can you believe that? But they're such an important part of your life, and so they're an equally important part of mine. You three are such an incredible family, and I'm so honored to get to be a part of it. King and I bonded over the past week, and I actually think we have a lot in common."

People laughed.

"We both can get a bit anxious. We both like to be silly! And, Erin, we both love you so much."

King heard the sound of several people saying, "Awww."

"I probably don't eat out of the trash *quite* as much." People laughed again. *Nice one*, King thought. Jin continued. "But, Erin, I'm just so inspired by how much you love Cleo and King, and I'm looking forward to making all three of you happy every day."

King saw that Erin was wiping happy tears away from her eyes. So were many other people in the yard. King thought that if dogs could cry, he might have cried too.

Instead, he just relaxed his whole body into the grass, let his tongue flop out of his mouth, and snuggled into Cleo's side.

"And I'm so glad my mom was able to make the long trip to be here to celebrate with us!" Jin finished. "Cheers, everyone!"

Jin's mom was sitting near King, and he watched her give a thumbs-up. Then she leaned over and gave both King and Cleo some enthusiastic pets.

King felt happier than he had in a long time. He watched as Jin sat down with his arm around Erin. They both looked so happy too.

My family may be changing, he thought, *but it's only going to get better.*

CHAPTER 14

WHAT DO YOU think, girl? This one ... or this one?"
Jasmine was holding two equally daring outfits.
It was Saturday morning, and Lulu had to decide what
she was going to wear to the wedding later that day.

Just last week, Lulu would have turned up her nose
at either one of the options—one was a lime-green tutu
with a paint splatter pattern, denim booties, and a plaid
beret, and the other was a bright blue pleather coat with
a feather headband—but today she could barely decide
which she loved more. Either way, she knew she was
going to make a splash. People would be talking about
her wedding look for dog years!

More important, she knew that no matter what she
wore to the wedding, she'd be wearing the best outfit of all: her confidence. Lulu would always be Lulu,
through good haircuts and bad; all she had to do was
believe in herself. After yesterday's adventure to find

King and her incredible rhymes in the Cat Battle, Lulu felt like she could take on any challenge that came her way. Plus, that groomer from Milan was right about one thing: Lulu *was* art. She didn't follow the trends, she set them! She was @LulusPerfectLife, after all!

Could any life truly be "perfect"? Lulu wondered as she pawed at the blue coat and headband, making her selection. *No, but when I'm truly being myself, I can come close!*

When they arrived at the wedding ceremony in Hugo's backyard, Lulu trotted right up to the front row and sat on a chair. She wanted to have a good view of Erin and Jin, and if she was being honest, she wanted them to have a good view of her too. The YouTube crew was up at the front as well, filming the wedding and getting some extra footage of Lulu, just like last night. She tried not to look into the camera, hoping they could grab some good candids.

"Lulu!" Jasmine nudged her. "You're *blowing up* on Instagram! Everyone loves your new look!"

The woman in the crew whose job was unclear must have overheard Jasmine, because Lulu heard a sudden "I can't," and soon the woman was over Jasmine's shoulder. She smiled, watching the likes quickly rack up under the photo.

"You know," the woman said, "Lulu's, like, the most photogenic dog we've ever worked with. She's bold, she's stylish, she's fearless. I simply can't. Maybe she should have a spin-off series!"

Lulu looked away, trying to seem like this was the most ordinary idea in the world, but inside, her heart was pounding. A whole spin-off series to herself would be a dream come true!

Then Jasmine took her place in front of the chairs, facing Lulu and the rest of the guests. With all of Lulu's worries over the past week, she had almost forgotten that Jasmine was officiating the wedding! It was a big honor for her best friend. Jasmine introduced the couple, and Lulu turned to watch as Erin and Jin walked down the aisle. They both looked gorgeous and so, so happy. Cleo walked in front of them, wearing a beautiful wreath of lilies, roses, and more. She was holding a flower basket in her mouth.

"Good job, flower girl!" Jasmine said when Cleo got to the front.

Lulu listened eagerly as Jasmine talked about Erin, and Jin, and love. She talked about the friends and family and neighbors who had come together to make this day so special.

"Erin takes care of all the dogs in the neighborhood, and she loves them so much," Jasmine said. "So we wanted to return that love and help you celebrate. And look, it's good luck to have 'something blue' at a wedding, right? Well, I think that might be Lulu!"

Erin pointed at Lulu, with her spiky blue hair and blue pleather outfit, and gave a big "woo!" Lulu knew that today wasn't about her, but in a way, wasn't every day *sort of* about her? Either way, it was always nice to get a shout-out.

Then Erin told Jin about how much she loved him, and Jin told Erin how much he loved her. Lulu didn't understand everything that was happening, but she knew it was simple, lovely, and #perfect.

"It's time for the rings!" Jasmine announced. Then she, Erin, and Jin turned their attention toward the aisle.

"Here, King! Here, boy!" Erin said, patting her leg. King slowly and carefully walked down the aisle. He had a small box attached to his collar, and he didn't even scratch at it or roll around on the ground trying to get it off. He just held his head high and walked right up to Erin and Jin. Lulu was impressed.

Jin looked impressed too as he took the ring box. He gave King some really nice pats on the head and scratches under the chin. "Great job, buddy! You did it," he said.

Lulu shared a look with Hugo, who was sitting in the grass nearby. They were both so proud of their friend. Then Jin and Erin put their new rings on each other's fingers and everybody cheered. They kissed, and ran back down the aisle, high-fiving everyone as Cleo and King followed behind.

It was time to party!

Hugo

HUGO SAT ON the porch with Lulu and King, looking out at the barbecue party. It had been a lot of fun—he'd even slow danced with Sofia! Up on his hind legs and everything! But now things were winding down, and he was a bit tired.

"It's nice to see Erin so happy," Hugo mused, and the others nodded in agreement. Then Hugo remembered something—his gift! He went into a nearby bush, picked up a large stick, climbed back onto the porch, and gave it to King.

"Could you give this to Erin?" Hugo asked.

"It's from both of us," Lulu added.

King nodded. "Will do! She's going to love this! She'll probably throw it away and ask me to return it!"

Hugo looked back into the yard. He thought about how nice it was to have all of his friends over, outside of Good Dogs. *We should do this more often,* he thought. He watched as Waffles ran around with Zoe. Napoleon, who was wearing a special bow tie for the occasion, was playing catch with Finn. Everyone was so happy, and it made Hugo happy too.

Everyone was facing Erin and Jin now, and Erin was talking to the guests and smiling ear to ear. Hugo could tell that the party had come to an end.

"Thank you so much for coming!" Erin said. "This was so much better than we ever could have hoped."

All the humans cheered and all the dogs barked for the newlywed couple as Erin scooped up King and Jin leashed up Cleo.

"Bye, King!" Lulu barked.

"Bye, guys!" King barked back.

As the happy family walked out of the yard, the wedding guests pulled out their brand-new bottles of purple bubble stuff! Erin and Jin must have bought more after the other day. Soon, the air was full of bubbles.

"Wow, this looks incredible," Lulu said. "I hope Jasmine is getting photos of me through the bubbles. I'll pose as if she is. Better safe than sorry."

As Lulu modeled for a camera that might or might not have been facing her, Hugo agreed about how great it all looked. Then he heard Waffles's voice. She was barking louder than he'd ever heard her bark.

"Bubbles! Bubbles! Bubbles! Did you see?! There's bubbles!"

Waffles ran as fast as she could toward the bubbles and jumped in the air, trying to catch as many in her mouth as she could.

Oh no! What's she doing? Hugo worried. He stood up, on alert. *Didn't she learn the first time? I swear, this puppy is going to be the end of me.*

He started walking toward Waffles so that he could intervene, but then Lulu shot him a pointed look. An especially pointed look, given her pointy haircut, he thought. Lulu knew him well, and Hugo could tell she knew he was getting worked up about Waffles again.

"She'll be fine," Lulu said reassuringly.

Hugo sighed. "You're right," he said, because he knew she was.

Down on the grass, Waffles was wiggling around, belly up, snatching bubbles out of the air with her tongue as they got close to the ground.

"Zoe! Come eat bubbles with me!" she yelped. "Bubbles are my favorite food!"

Lulu and Hugo laughed. Then Lulu turned to Hugo. "What do you think you'll do with your free time?" she asked. "Now that you won't be constantly worrying about Waffles?"

"Oh, I have some ideas," Hugo said, and he looked at a spot on the porch where a lovely late-afternoon sunbeam was starting to form.

Jasmine walked over and set her purse down. Lulu happily climbed inside, said goodbye to Hugo, and was carried away.

"See ya later, Lu!" he called after her. Then he watched the rest of the guests clear out of his yard. In the spot where Hugo and Enrique used to play tug-of-war with a Frisbee, Waffles was having some sort of contest with Zoe. They were both running and jumping, and having the best time.

"Hey, bud! Here, Hugo!" Enrique called as he walked into the house, and so Hugo followed. In the kitchen, Enrique gave Hugo his favorite treat, then some really great belly rubs. Hugo wished it would never end, but unfortunately . . .

"Sorry, buddy, I've got some homework to finish up," Enrique said. Then Hugo saw him look around the kitchen to make sure his mom and dad weren't looking. He opened the cabinet and gave Hugo *another* treat, with one last pat on the head.

Wow, what a day, Hugo thought. Then he walked into the living room and hopped up onto the edge of the couch by the bookshelf, where the perfect sunbeam had made its way through the front window. He settled down and looked out to the street. He liked the way the sun made the fur on his legs look even more golden than usual . . .

One car, he noticed with a yawn. *Two* . . .

Then he closed his eyes. He could feel himself starting to fall asleep, which of course was how all the best naps started.

CHAPTER 15

KING YAWNED AND stretched his legs. It had been a long day, and an even longer week, and he was ready to fall asleep.

"Bedtime! Let's get some rest," Cleo said, and he followed her into their bedroom.

"Whoa," he exclaimed, looking around the room. "Everything is different!"

King couldn't believe his eyes. Someone had re-arranged the entire room so that Jin's office was on one side and the dog beds and toys were on the other, with a bookshelf separating the two areas. Not to mention, the dogs' area looked way nicer than before, with new fuzzy blankets and plush pillows.

"Wow! Feel this, Cleo!" King called out as he flopped into his bed. "It's softer than . . . than . . . something really, really soft."

She nodded as she cuddled up on her own new blanket.

There were no more boxes or pieces of computer equipment blocking his bed, and he was able to lie down more comfortably than ever. He glanced out the window, and now that Jin's desk had been moved over, he could see the moon perfectly. And that was the most comforting thing of all.

There you are, old friend, King thought as he stared at the moon.

"You like?"

King turned to see Jin's mom standing in the doorway.

"I thought you might like," she said.

King stood up and wagged his tail like a maniac. "Cleo! She rearranged the room for us!" he said. "Can you believe it?"

King felt so thankful, he couldn't contain himself. He ran right up to Jin's mom, stood up and leaned on her legs, and gave her as many grateful smooches as he could. She laughed and petted him all over his body. Cleo sauntered over, and Jin's mom petted her too.

"Yes, yes . . . good dogs!"

It was a sweet moment. And to King's delight, it got even sweeter. Jin's mom sneakily glanced over her shoulder, then opened her hand to reveal two crunchy treats. King and Cleo both eagerly devoured them.

King was licking the palm of her hand when Jin walked in, laughing. "Don't spoil them too much, Mom," he said, hugging her.

"Okay, okay," she said reluctantly. "Good night."

But as soon as she was gone, Jin opened his own hand to reveal even more treats. The soft and chewy kind.

Mmm, King thought as he nibbled out of Jin's hand. *Two kinds of treats in one night.*

"You both were just perfect today," Jin said, sitting down on the floor to pet King and Cleo. "Who's a perfect doggy? Who's a perfect doggy?"

King looked at Cleo. Cleo looked back at King.

Who's he talking about here? King wondered.

"Both of you are!" Jin said, giving them both even more pets. "So, listen. With my job, I can't get time off for a honeymoon right now, but don't worry. We're planning a big camping trip for all four of us! Next month. It'll be so fun. We'll sleep in tents, and go hiking and canoeing—King, have you ever been in a canoe?"

King looked up, over Jin's shoulder, to see Erin standing in the doorway. She was smiling.

"Are you talking to the dogs?" she asked Jin, surprising him. He must have thought he was alone.

"Yeah. Yeah, I am," he said.

"I love that," she said with a laugh, and she sat down next to him. Now King and Cleo were getting major rubdowns from both Jin and Erin. King rolled over onto his back so they could rub his tummy. He used to think that there was nothing better than a belly rub, but lately he was beginning to realize that there actually was: a belly rub from two people at the same time. He liked to call this move the "four-hand massage," and he was getting a really great one right now.

That's probably the best thing about having a new family member, King thought as he snuggled up between Erin and Jin. *More pets, pats, rubs, and scratches.*

Then his mouth began to water as he smelled something special in Erin's hand.

And more T-R-E-A-T-S!

ABOUT THE ILLUSTRATOR

TOR FREEMAN (@tormalore) was born in London and received a degree in illustration from Kingston University. She has written and illustrated many children's books and was awarded a Sendak Fellowship in 2012. Tor has also been published in magazines and taught art to students of all ages.

ABOUT THE AUTHORS

RACHEL WENITSKY (@RachelWenitsky) is a comedy writer and actor who has written for *The Tonight Show Starring Jimmy Fallon*, *Saturday Night Live*, and *Reductress*. She is the head writer and a co-host of *The Story Pirates Podcast*, a kids and family podcast on Gimlet Media.

DAVID SIDOROV (@DavidSidorov) is a comedy writer and director who has written for *Alternatino with Arturo Castro*, *Odd Mom Out*, *The Gong Show*, *Billy on the Street*, and *Holey Moley*. He was a field producer and director on *The Rundown with Robin Thede*, and was formerly a writer and director at *The Onion*.

Rachel and David are a married couple living in Brooklyn, New York. They do not have a dog at the time of writing these bios, but hope that they will by the time you're reading this!

DON'T MISS

GOOD DOGS on a BAD DAY
Sometimes taking risks pays off,
but sometimes it leads to disaster.

And coming soon!

GOOD DOGS in BAD SWEATERS
The holidays can be rough for pups.